THE MAGICAL BOOKSHOP 2

G000136850

BROUGHT

to

BOOK

LIZ HEDGECOCK

WHITE
RHINO
BOOKS

For Paula,
my book bestie

'Lights!' called Jemma.

Raphael approached the bank of switches, screwed up his face, and remaining at arm's-length, flicked one on. Overhead, the iron chandelier lit up without a flicker.

Jemma laughed. 'It's perfectly safe.'

'Then why are you standing all the way over there?' asked Raphael.

'Fine.' Jemma rolled her eyes, walked across to the light panel and switched on the remaining eleven lamps in one go. The huge lower floor of the bookshop was bathed in warm light, and the sinister shadows Jemma remembered from their first foray down the stone steps were a thing of the past. Now the huge room looked grand; majestic, even.

'Wow,' breathed Carl. 'It's something when you see it all put together, isn't it?' He shot Jemma an admiring glance, and she tried not to preen.

'It is, rather,' she said, and smiled.

In some ways it had been much easier than she thought to get the space renovated. The cathedral crypt, as it had been, was sound, watertight and pest free, which had spoiled the fun of their tradespeople considerably. Apart from getting electricity and water put in, most of their time was focused on buying furniture and fittings, and giving what was already there a good clean.

And that was where Carl had got involved.

It had begun when Jemma, exhausted after a morning downstairs removing centuries of grime from the stone floor, had called into Rolando's for a panini and a double espresso. Carl had done a double-take when she presented herself at the counter and gave her order.

'Not a cappuccino?' he asked.

'Not today,' said Jemma.

He continued to gaze at her, and she realised from his expression that she possibly should have checked her appearance before venturing out. She felt sweat in the small of her back, and suspected that the dirt on her clothes, while possibly antique, was not a look favoured by the majority of Rolando's customers. 'Don't worry, I'm taking it away,' she said, blushing.

'Never mind that,' said Carl, putting the panini in to warm. 'What have you been doing?'

'Cleaning,' said Jemma. 'Raphael and I are taking turns.'

To give Raphael credit, he was putting in some work. Admittedly, if ever Jemma went downstairs during one of his cleaning shifts, she often found him leaning on his mop and reading a book. But when he came upstairs and she took over, he had always managed to get a lot done.

Carl put a disposable cup under the coffee machine. Then he turned back to her, and leaned forward. 'Do you need any help?' he muttered.

'Oh heck, yes,' said Jemma. 'You've seen it.' She had invited Carl to pop round one day when he had finished his shift, and he had marvelled at the high ceilings, the pillars, and the intricate stone carvings. Taken as a whole, it was an amazing room. Up close, though, it was decidedly dirty. *Then again*, Jemma thought, *if I hadn't had a shower for five hundred years or so, I probably wouldn't look my best either.*

'I can ask Raphael, if you like,' she said. 'Aren't you busy here?'

Carl eyed the queue and grinned. 'Yeah, but extra money is always handy. The theatre I was ushering at closed.'

'Oh, I see,' said Jemma. Carl always appeared so contented when she saw him that she had never really thought about him outside the café.

'Yeah,' said Carl. 'And I took that on because I was resting between acting jobs. Anyway, better get on or I'll be out of this one as well.' He gave her a tight little smile, and put her panini on the counter.

So Carl had come to do three hours' cleaning downstairs when he finished at Rolando's. Jemma always took him downstairs, made sure he had everything he needed, and brought him tea and biscuits halfway through

3

his shift. She had hoped that they would get chatting, and she would get to know him better. But he was focused on the job, and disinclined to be communicative. She longed to ask him about the acting jobs he had had, and whether she might have seen him in anything, but she sensed that would be an awkward question. Anyway, she had things to do upstairs.

But now the crypt was irreproachably clean, and fitted out with light-oak bookshelves and comfortable old armchairs. That accounted for two-thirds of the room. The rest, following negotiations, had become a café.

Jemma had always imagined having a café as part of the space, though she realised it would be in direct competition with Rolando's. It had been Raphael, surprisingly, who suggested discussing it with Rolando. 'I don't want to tread on any toes,' he said, 'but it strikes me that there could be advantage on both sides.'

Jemma had gaped at him. 'Will you be all ruthless again, like you were with Brian?'

Raphael laughed. 'Not at all,' he said. 'And Rolando is rather a different proposition from Brian, although not necessarily easier to deal with. I'll pop in when the lunchtime rush is over, and see if I can get an audience.'

He had returned fifteen minutes later with the news that Rolando would call round at about four.

Jemma had waited with bated breath. Even though she was busy in the shop, the hands of the clock still crawled round. Then at four o'clock precisely, as she was putting *Men Are From Mars, Women Are From Venus* into a bag, a small dark-haired woman erupted into the shop, fixed beady black eyes on her, and demanded 'Where is Raphael?'

'Oh, I think he's in the back somewhere,' said Jemma. 'Shall I call him?'

The woman walked straight into the back room as if it were the obvious thing to do, and called out 'Raphael? Dove sei?'

'Ciao, Giulia,' Raphael replied from the stockroom, and came out. 'We're just popping downstairs, Jemma,' he called, and she heard footsteps which were quickly drowned by a stream of rapid Italian. Jemma looked after them for several seconds, even though she could see nothing and hear little more, and only a discreet cough from her customer recalled her to what she was meant to be doing.

Half an hour later the footsteps travelled the other way, again accompanied by voluble Italian, but this time Raphael was saying at least as much as Giulia was. The meeting ended in the back room, where Giulia gave Raphael a firm handshake, then scurried out.

Jemma didn't get a chance to ask about the outcome until they closed at five. 'Go on, then,' she said, as Raphael turned the sign from *Open* to *Closed*. 'What happened?'

'Oh, but don't you want to cash up first, Jemma?' Raphael's eyes twinkled with evil mischief.

Jemma drew herself up to her full five feet two. 'No, I do not, and you know it. Come on, Raphael, spill.'

'Oh, very well.' Raphael sat down in the armchair, and Folio jumped into his lap. 'So, what Rolando and I have agreed—'

Jemma's eyes narrowed. 'But that wasn't Rolando. I heard you call her Giulia.'

'Yes,' said Raphael. 'It's complicated, and I'll explain in a minute. Anyway, what Rolando has agreed is that they will rent the café space from me for an agreed amount, paid monthly, and that they will offer drinks and hot and cold snacks, prepared in the main shop. Oh, and cake, of course. They will provide a coffee machine and the heating and serving equipment, and I shall provide tables and chairs. One of their staff will run the café, and they will remain an employee of Rolando's.'

'That sounds sensible,' said Jemma. 'Do we get to choose who they send?'

Raphael smiled. 'I did suggest that, as we know Carl best, and he has helped us out already, he would be a good fit. Providing he is receptive to the idea, of course. And Rolando seems happy with that.'

Jemma couldn't help executing a little round of applause.

'I'm glad you approve,' said Raphael, drily.

'Oh, I do,' said Jemma. 'But tell me about Rolando. Or Giulia.'

'There isn't much to tell,' said Raphael. 'Rolando's opened in, what, the nineties. The bookshop was going through a difficult time, so I didn't really pay much attention. There might have been a Rolando, there might not. In any case, Giulia has always insisted that the café is called Rolando's, and that Rolando makes the business decisions. Behind closed doors, where it doesn't matter, she answers to Giulia. Everywhere else, she is representing

Rolando.'

'What happened, do you think?' asked Jemma.

'I used to wonder about that,' said Raphael. 'Then I realised it was none of my business, and it was up to Giulia to decide how she did things.'

Jemma bit her lip at the implied rebuke. 'Well, I'm glad it's sorted,' she said. 'Let's get on and cash up.'

After that, time had flown; working with Jim from James's Antique Emporium, who had found them classic bentwood tables and chairs, moving the fiction section downstairs, and restocking a shop at least twice its previous size, at the same time as continuing to serve their ever-increasing customer base. There were days when Jemma found herself putting the key into the front door of her flat, unsure how she had got there, or woke up on the sofa as light crept through the gap in the curtains. *But it was all worth it,* she thought, gazing around her at the beautiful room, the gleaming café counter, and of course, the books.

Today was the grand reopening. They had closed the shop for the morning to put the finishing touches to it all, and the hands of the huge railway clock on the wall showed one minute to twelve. She ticked *Lights* on her list, and looked up at Raphael. 'Are you ready?' she asked.

Raphael raised his eyebrows. 'We open the shop every morning, Jemma.'

Jemma sighed. 'Are you ready, Carl?'

Carl adjusted the bib of his apron, and grinned. 'I'm ready,' he said.

Jemma took a deep breath. 'In that case,' she said, 'it's

showtime.' She ran upstairs and into the main shop, and grinned at the crowd peering through the shop window. Then she turned the shop sign around, and flung the door wide open.

As Jemma had expected, she saw familiar faces in the stream of people who rushed through the doors of the shop. The two Golden Age crime fans were there, and the man with an inexhaustible appetite for books about railways, and the woman, now out of hospital, whose sister had come in search of *Jane Eyre* on Jemma's first day, and who was working through Mrs Gaskell. 'Where is the fiction section?' she asked, stopping dead and staring at the place where it had been, now occupied by Cookery, Craft, and Travel.

'Don't worry,' said Jemma, smiling. 'It's moved downstairs and expanded.'

And expanded it had. When the new oak bookshelves arrived, Raphael had gasped in horror, convinced that Jemma had ordered double what was needed. But once the van men had got them all downstairs, he wondered audibly whether they had quite enough.

'We can always order more,' said Jemma. 'Anyway, better to have too many books for the shelves than too many shelves for the books.'

But it felt like a close-run thing at times. They had packed up and brought down the fiction books on the shelves upstairs, and using the calculation that one full box of books equalled one shelf of a bookcase, Jemma had worked out that they would fill about a third of the space. 'We need more fiction!' she had cried, and rushed upstairs to the stockroom.

Luckily the bookshop agreed with her, delivering box after box of novels, mostly in complete sets. 'Thank you,' whispered Jemma, time after time, as she unpacked boxes of Stephen King, Terry Pratchett, and Nora Roberts. Quite apart from the time saved in sorting and alphabetising, she was relieved that the shop seemed content with their plans, and even inclined to encourage them.

Once or twice, as she unpacked boxes, Jemma had caught Carl looking first puzzled, then suspicious. 'Jemma,' he said, as she unpacked a complete *Forsyte Saga*, 'how do you know what's in the boxes?'

'I don't,' said Jemma.

'Oh,' said Carl. 'Isn't that a bit . . . odd?'

'What, that we don't label the boxes when they go into the stockroom?' said Jemma.

Carl's face lit up. 'Exactly! I mean, imagine if I opened a box expecting it to be chocolate chips, and it turned out to be sun-dried tomatoes?'

'You're absolutely right,' said Jemma, and opened a

box which was full of Anne McCaffreys. She looked up, and saw Carl watching her.

'You weren't expecting that, were you?' he said, accusingly.

'I wasn't expecting anything, really,' said Jemma. 'I just have faith that we've got enough fiction books in our stockroom to fill up the shelves.'

Carl sighed, and carried on filling the cupboard behind the counter with boxes of sugar lumps, individually wrapped coffee biscuits, and reams of paper napkins. Jemma could tell that he wasn't satisfied with her explanation, but what else could she say? How could she explain the vagaries of the bookshop? *You'll get used to it, just as I did*, she said to herself, and carried on shelving.

Customers continued to stream past her, all following the arrows through the back room to the stairs. Jemma had kept a tally in her head as people passed her, and she reckoned that she was up to about a hundred and eighty. The council had recommended that they limit numbers downstairs to two hundred, which at the time she had thought ridiculously unachievable. She shook her head in disbelief. *Twenty more, then people will have to wait*, she told herself. The stream was beginning to slow as she counted another ten, then another five. At last, a pause of perhaps ten seconds, then a couple came hurrying through the door. 'Is it today?' they asked. 'The opening?'

'Yes, it is,' said Jemma. 'We're almost full, so you're just in time. If you follow the others, you can see the new room downstairs.'

They hurried off, closely followed by an elderly man

with a string shopping bag.

'Um, Jemma.' Raphael was standing in the Science section, looking perturbed.

'Hi, Raphael,' she said. 'How's it going down there?'

'It's busy,' he said.

'Good busy?' said Jemma, as a man in a suit strode by in a purposeful manner.

'Yes, good busy,' said Raphael. 'But *busy*. You should go down and see.'

'I thought you'd never ask,' said Jemma, grinning.

'Er, excuse me?' said a timid voice behind her.

A pale, thin young man stood on the step, dressed in a black raincoat, black beanie hat, black jeans and sunglasses. 'Hello!' she cried. 'Are you coming in?'

'I wasn't sure if I could,' said the young man, shifting from foot to foot. 'I thought it might be invitation-only.'

'Everyone's invited,' said Jemma. 'Well, until we're full, at any rate. And you're the last customer we can allow in, so you'd better hurry.'

'Yes, do come in,' said Raphael. He looked at Jemma hopefully. 'So does that mean that I can't let anyone else into the shop?'

'That's exactly it,' said Jemma. 'Not till people start leaving. One out, one in.'

'That makes things considerably easier,' said Raphael. He dashed behind the counter, pulled a sheet of paper from one of the drawers, wrote *Currently Full – Please Wait To Be Admitted* in his flowing copperplate, and stuck it in the middle of the shop window with sticky tape. 'There,' he said, picked up his newspaper, and collapsed into the armchair.

'Don't get too comfortable,' warned Jemma. 'If the queue gets too big at the downstairs till, I may send them up to you.'

Raphael lowered the newspaper until his eyes were visible, then rolled them at her. 'If you could give me five minutes first, I'd appreciate that.'

'See you later,' said Jemma. The young man was still standing there, watching them. Jemma noticed that he now had a copy of *Databases for Beginners* in his hand. 'Would you like to come downstairs and see the new book room?' she asked.

'Oh, um, yes please,' said the young man.

'Come along, then,' said Jemma. She led the way downstairs, reflecting that it was nice to have a customer who waited to be asked, rather than plunging among the books and luxuriating in them in the messy manner that so many people did. She had a feeling that this customer, if he took a book from the shelf then decided against it, would replace it exactly where he had found it.

'Watch out,' she warned him, as they approached the large oak door. 'It may be a little crowded.' She felt as if she were warning herself, too.

But nothing prepared her for the swarm of people downstairs. Some customers were doing what she had expected; sitting or standing in the café area chatting and enjoying the range of canapés which had come from Rolando's that morning. Other customers seeking a proper lunch queued up nicely at the café counter, where Carl seemed his usual unflappable self.

But the bookshop area was in a state of polite chaos. Customers were wandering from shelf to shelf, or standing in the middle of aisles, reading. Several already carried piles of books. And most of them were chatting, or calling friends over to look at what they had found. The effect was of a hive of companionable bees.

'I'd better get to the till,' said Jemma. She excuse-med her way through the knots of people, having to stop several times and accept compliments, and eventually slipped behind the shop counter with a sigh of relief. 'Till's open!' she called, and a couple of the more suggestible customers actually wandered across, eyes slightly glazed, chins on their piles of books.

Jemma was kept busy ringing up purchases for the next few minutes. A couple of customers did leave; but most of them wandered back towards the café area. The rest seemed in no hurry to finish browsing, or chatting. In a rare lull she looked past the queue to the shelves. Some of them already had considerable gaps showing.

Briefly, she panicked. *How do we keep up?* Then she remembered Raphael, with his own till upstairs, and relief broke over her like day. She served her next customer, then climbed on the wooden chair they had put behind the counter for slack periods and waved her arms for attention.

'Customers!' she shouted. 'If you wish to make a purchase, and you're not currently in the queue, please go to the till upstairs. I'm closing this till in a few minutes so that I can fetch more books.'

She heard muttering, but it remained low-level.

'Bit busier than you expected?' said Mohammed,

putting two RK Narayan novels on the counter.

'Just a bit,' said Jemma. She had persuaded Raphael to let her order a box of a hundred large paper bags with handles, and their level was already diminishing. 'That's five pounds, please. Cash or card?'

Mohammed grinned. 'Phone,' he said. He paid, then wandered towards the café.

Jemma had a sudden vision of herself trapped in the crypt for eternity, with customers who never left but merely moved to different parts of the room; browsing the books, buying the books, going to the café, then wandering back to the shelves.

'I need a big bag if you've got one,' said the next customer, a harassed-looking woman in a floral dress, putting a stack of eight books on the counter.

'That's fine,' said Jemma, pulling a large paper bag from the box and checking each book as she slipped it inside. 'That will be twenty pounds, please.'

It'll be fine, she told herself, as the customer rooted through her handbag, pulled out her purse, put a ten and a five-pound note on the counter, and began counting out coins. *Of course it's busy on the first day. That's what you wanted. That's why you did the window display, and ran a countdown on social media, and made sure that all our regulars knew. It won't be like this every day. Apart from anything else, this lot are buying enough books to keep them going for a good month, if not more.*

'And that makes twenty,' said the customer, putting down a five-pence piece, two tuppences and a penny and closing her purse with a snap.

'Lovely, thank you,' said Jemma, counting the bits of change into the right compartments of the till. Not that that would do much good when Raphael had put everything everywhere, but still. She had standards. 'Next please,' she said, and counted three more customers behind the man who stepped up with an armful of Robert Harris.

Four more to serve, then she could scurry upstairs to the stockroom and begin refilling the shelves. And once the canapés and complimentary drinks ran out, people would leave. They must have places to be, after all. *You can handle this, Jemma*, she told herself, and beamed a confident, happy smile at her customer, who looked, if anything, rather taken aback.

Chapter 3

Despite keeping up a stream of positive internal self-talk as she dealt with the remainder of the queue, Jemma was still very glad to serve the last person. 'Back in five minutes!' she shouted, and dashed out from behind the counter.

'Jemma!' She turned to see Carl, coffee pot in one hand, cloth in the other, looking terrified.

She hurried over. 'What is it?'

'Don't leave me!'

'I have to,' she said quietly. 'We need more books.'

'What if they start coming to me with them?'

'Then send them to Raphael. If they have book questions, send them to Raphael. I'll be gone for five minutes, I promise.' But as she weaved her way through the customers Jemma didn't see all the boxes of lovely books which she would bring down and open, but Carl's agonised face.

Upstairs, she almost collided with the back of the queue for the till. She thought briefly about asking Raphael how it was going, then decided that would be unwise, at best. Instead she wrenched open the door to the stockroom, closed it behind her, and leaned against it, panting.

What have we unleashed? Then she told herself that she was being silly, grabbed the first box she saw, took it to the top of the stairs, and went back for another. She had to go further into the room this time, because more and more of the shelves were growing bare. 'We have to get more stock,' she said, out loud. *But when?* She brushed the thought aside for now, and took another box outside. When she did, she found that the first box had vanished.

'Has anyone seen my box?' she asked the queue.

'I think it went thataway,' said a cheery red-faced man, pointing towards the main shop.

Jemma sighed, and walked in to find the box open on the counter and three customers adding books to their piles. 'Leave some for the rest of us,' said a woman further down the queue.

'Those are supposed to be for downstairs,' said Jemma, but nobody took any notice. Raphael was busy with the cash register, and had co-opted Mohammed to pack books for him. Mohammed looked very cheerful; Raphael decidedly less so.

'Should I ask?' asked Jemma.

Raphael, tight-lipped, shook his head. 'Later,' he said.

So Jemma returned to the stockroom, and this time carried each box individually to the lower floor and put it behind the café counter. 'Don't let anyone get at them,' she told Carl.

On her way upstairs she almost fell over a group of customers crouching on the floor and worshipping Folio, who was purring and waving his tail as if this was perfectly normal. He did look particularly large and sleek today, and his orange fur glowed in the lamplight as if he had been polished for the occasion. 'Be good, Folio,' she called as she passed, and he flicked his tail as if to say that she didn't need to remind a cat with such impeccable manners. Still, he appeared happy enough, so off Jemma went.

One more box, she told herself, *and that's it. And if we run out of books, we'll just have to close early.*

She carried the last box down, put it on the shop counter, and got out her scissors. Within she found a stack of Isaac Asimov books, and heaved a sigh of relief. She took the box to the right section, began shelving, and soon found herself surrounded by a group of people clearly waiting for her to finish so that they could undo her good work. After a minute or two, feeling eyes on the back of her neck, she asked, 'Would it be easier if I left the box for you?'

Multiple nods.

Jemma sighed. 'Fine. I'll come back in a few minutes and shelve anything you don't want, then.'

She took her scissors to the café counter and attacked the next box. 'I've never seen anything like it,' said Carl, staring at the masses buzzing around the shelves. 'It's like the January sales.'

'I guess this is what success looks like,' said Jemma. But as she said it, she felt strangely flat.

19

Carl shrugged, poured out two Americanos, and slid them across the counter. 'Maybe. Whatever it is, it's exhausting.'

Jemma opened the next box. 'Oh gosh,' she said. Inside were rows and rows of Chalet School stories. 'I remember these! They spoke a different language every day, and they never did any work.' She grinned. 'I have a feeling these won't last long.' She carried the box to Children's Fiction, put it on the floor, yelled 'Chalet School!', and took a step back as women hurried from all around.

Then she heard raised voices from the Science Fiction shelves. 'I think you'll find that this is mine now,' said a bald-headed man in a black T-shirt.

'You've already got five,' said a woman with tortoiseshell-framed glasses and bright-red hair. 'I really want this one. You're just picking them up.'

The man's nose wrinkled. 'I don't see how you've reached that conclusion,' he said. 'Speed doesn't necessarily equate to lack of discrimination. In other words: you snooze, you lose.' And he added the book to his pile with a smug smile.

'Is everything all right here?' said Jemma.

The red-haired woman flung out an accusing finger. 'He took my book! I was reaching for it, and he snatched it from right under my nose!'

Jemma looked at the book, then at the shelves. 'There's another copy,' she said, pointing.

'But I wanted that edition!' wailed the woman. 'With that cover!'

The bald-headed man sighed, took the other book off

the shelf, and gave her his copy. 'If it's that important,' he said wearily. 'Honestly, Felicity, what a fuss over nothing.'

'Wait a minute,' said Jemma. 'Do you two know each other?'

The woman sniffed. 'In a manner of speaking.' She paused. 'But thank you, Jerome,' she said, and gave him a shy little smile.

Jemma walked off, shaking her head at the absurdity of people. But she hadn't walked far when she heard an '*Ow!*'

Potential catastrophes flashed before her eyes. A heavy book on the head? A hot coffee scald? She hurried to the source of the noise, and found the pale young man sucking his forefinger and staring at a hissing Folio. 'What happened?'

'He scratched me,' said the young man. At least, Jemma thought that was what he said, as he hadn't removed his finger from his mouth.

'Is that right?' she asked Folio, who had fluffed up in rage and now appeared twice his normal size.

Folio glared at her with eyes that were almost all black pupil, but was silent.

'Oh dear,' said Jemma. 'May I see?'

The young man took his finger from his mouth and held it out to Jemma, looking resolutely away.

Jemma, knowing Folio as well as she did, had expected a wound of some magnitude; what she was presented with resembled a paper cut. 'That doesn't seem too bad,' she said. 'It isn't bleeding—'

The young man shuddered. 'Good,' he said.

'I bet it hurts, though,' she said, to save his dignity.

'And of course, Folio shouldn't have done it.' She glared at Folio, who blinked. 'Were you stroking him at the time?'

'No,' said the young man, looking anywhere but at Folio. 'That is, I was going to, and I reached down, and – then it happened.'

'I'm afraid he's probably a bit over-excited today, what with all the people,' said Jemma. 'He's normally a very nice cat. Aren't you, Folio?'

Folio gazed up at her with innocent eyes, his paws placed neatly together.

'I'll get this cleaned, just in case, and put a plaster on, then you'll be fine.' She gave his arm a reassuring pat. 'Come upstairs and I'll get the first-aid kit. Folio, if you're going to be grumpy, take a time out.'

Folio interpreted this as an instruction to jump on the shop counter. Jemma sighed, and led the way upstairs.

She might have been imagining it, but the queue in the shop seemed a little shorter. Jemma retrieved the first-aid kit from under the sink, opened the stockroom door, and beckoned the young man in. 'This is probably the quietest place in the shop at the moment,' she said.

'Wow,' he replied. 'I mean, I thought you had a lot of books. I didn't realise there was this, as well.'

'It is quite something,' said Jemma proudly.

'And this is all books?' He took off his sunglasses. His eyes were pale green, like sea-glass.

'Yes,' said Jemma, 'all books. Now, do you think we should wash this?' She examined the finger in question.

'No, it'll be fine,' said the young man. 'I think it was the shock.'

'Mmm,' said Jemma. 'Well, keep an eye on it.' She squeezed antiseptic cream on the place where Folio had broken the skin, and rubbed it in. 'Would you like a plaster? I'm afraid we've only got Mr Bump ones.'

The young man nodded, and Jemma carefully wrapped a plaster around his finger. 'There you go,' she said, 'all done.'

'Thank you,' said the young man. Jemma noticed that he looked slightly less pale than he had before. Perhaps he really had been suffering from shock.

'Would you like a cup of tea?' she asked. 'Or a biscuit?'

'Oh no, I'd better go,' he said, heading for the door. 'I need to be somewhere, that is, I mean—' He glanced at the book in his hand.

'Don't worry about that,' said Jemma. 'You can have that for free, as an apology from Folio. And me.'

'Can I?' He smiled. 'Thank you.' He had an unexpectedly nice smile, if a little toothy.

'Don't mention it,' said Jemma, and held the door open for him. 'Folio-related injury,' she muttered in Raphael's direction, as she escorted the young man from the shop.

Downstairs things were still busy, but less frantic than before. The customers were more inclined to sit in the café with a drink, or settle in an armchair and read a book. But they were still coming to the counter with purchases, of course, and Jemma was kept very busy. She used all the big paper bags; she ran dangerously low on the normal-sized bags, and had to send Carl to the stockroom for another box. At least he looked less hunted and more cheerful, now that the earlier rush had died down.

At half past four Jemma had just finished serving a customer when an ostentatious throat-clearing behind her made her stub her toe on the counter. 'I think we should close early today,' said Raphael. 'I suggest a quarter to.'

Jemma eyed the scene before her. Apart from the queue, they were down to about ten customers who wandered aimlessly around the bookshelves, as if they were lost in a labyrinth of books and had forgotten their ball of string. 'You're right,' she said. 'Fifteen minutes till closing, everyone!' she shouted.

Raphael winced. 'I do wish you'd warn me, Jemma.'

'Sorry, forgot,' said Jemma, cheerfully. Actually, she had forgotten that she *could* shout like that. Four years of careful corporate self-presentation had almost taken it out of her.

At length the last customer was served, the last book bagged, and the last money placed in the till. Jemma saw the last two customers upstairs and out of the shop, and turned the sign to *Closed* with a feeling of great relief. 'Well,' she said, 'what did you think of our reopening?'

Raphael sagged like a puppet whose master had gone on holiday. Carl was in slightly better condition; but his shoulders sagged, and the corners of his mouth did too.

'I know it was tiring, but it's opening day,' she said. 'Of course it was going to be busy—'

'How do we know it won't always be this busy?' said Carl, and Raphael gave him a grateful look.

'He's right,' he said. 'We only opened at midday, and we're exhausted. Imagine if it's like this again tomorrow.'

'It won't be,' said Jemma. 'And we can put systems in

place to manage capacity. I could bring down more stock before we open, and then it will be much easier to fill the shelves. And maybe Carl could help in the shop when the café's quiet.'

Carl's eyes widened in a way that suggested that he was not on board with this idea.

'Anyway,' said Jemma, 'it will all be much easier when the lift is put in.'

Raphael was silent for a moment, thinking. A meow from the back room made them turn. Folio strolled in, hopped into the armchair, flopped down, and closed his eyes.

'That might help,' said Raphael. 'I agree that we can't predict how busy the shop will be every day. But we *will* be busier. We *will* need more books, which means that someone – me – must go out and find them. And if we couldn't keep on top of things with you, me and Carl in the shop today, what will it be like if I'm out on a book-buying expedition? Or one of you has a day off, or rings in sick? No, I've decided.' He drew himself up and looked at them both. 'We must hire another member of staff, and the sooner the better.'

Jemma told herself, as she stood on the tube with her nose millimetres away from someone's back, that she only felt defeated because she was tired. It was probably true. She hadn't slept well the night before, it had certainly been a stressful day, and they had had no breaks from the grand opening until the shop was closed.

And that hadn't been a break, as such. Admittedly, Carl had made tea, and they had shared the last two cakes from the café, which had been delicious. But all the time, an air of oppression had hung over them.

Cashing up ought to have been a triumphant occasion. They reviewed the transactions on the card machines, then counted up and bagged the money in the three tills. The shop had never known a day like it. Raphael was actually nervous about leaving so much money in the safe overnight. 'I'll take Rolando's share round first thing tomorrow, then I'm heading to the bank,' he said, slamming the door of the safe and turning the dial quickly, as if it might bite him. And again, the joy that they should have felt became fear, and mistrust.

Jemma had to admit, glancing around the near-empty shelves, the books left on the floor, and the cake crumbs and occasional teaspoons which littered the café, that it had come at a cost. 'We'll get you cleaned up,' she said, to no one in particular, and got the broom out of the small cupboard near the equally diminutive customer toilets. *Raphael is right. We need help.*

So why don't I like the idea? She swayed gently with the motion of the train and bumped against a man in a leather jacket whose large headphones rendered him oblivious. *Why does it bother me?* She closed her eyes, tuned out the faint thumping coming from the leather-jacketed man, and tried to concentrate.

You failed, said a chirpy little voice. *You couldn't manage it all. You fell short.*

Jemma frowned. *How could I have known it would go so well? No one could have predicted it would be so busy.*

But you wanted it to be, said the annoying little voice. *You set things up to make sure that it was. And then you couldn't follow through.*

Jemma squeezed her eyes shut. *It was mostly fine,* she insisted, feeling injured. *OK, so Folio scratched that man, but it was only a little scratch, and I sorted it out.*

Two customers nearly came to blows over a book. Raphael actually had to grab one of the customers to pack books for him. The voice paused. Jemma wouldn't have

27

thought it was possible to pause in a smug manner, but the voice managed it. *Rather unprofessional, don't you think?*

Jemma was about to reply in her head when the train forestalled her by announcing her stop. She opened her eyes, squeezed through the press of commuters, and popped onto the platform, surprised, as usual, by the fresh September air.

She was sorely tempted to stop in at the takeaway. *Stay strong, Jemma*, she told herself, turning her head away from the bright lights, the neon, and the enticing smells. Besides, she had picked up the ingredients for spaghetti carbonara from the mini-market, as well as a two-glass bottle of wine. A hard day was no reason to lose one's self control.

She let herself into the townhouse, walked slowly up all the flights of stairs – there seemed at least twice as many as usual after the day she'd had – and gazed at the front door of her flat. One day she would get a screwdriver, and put that *B* on straight. It irritated her beyond words every time she saw it, but somehow there was never time. Or a screwdriver.

Jemma hung her bag on the back of the door, changed her boots for the padded slippers she had treated herself to a month before, and took the food into the kitchenette. The cupboards were still a bit too far up on the wall, and the worktop was too high, but at least she could afford nice olive oil now, and Parmesan cheese. Jemma switched on the radio, got herself a glass of squash (wine was to go with dinner), opened *Italian Food for Beginners*, and set to work.

Over the last month or so, cooking her own meals had gone from being a laborious exercise with often surprising and atypical results to something which, usually, tasted quite nice. She had even come to find it therapeutic at the end of a long day. A chance to turn events over in her mind, and think about how she should have responded, or what she could have done better. But this evening, as she sweated garlic in a pan and chopped bacon into little pieces, she was too tired to beat herself up. *I'll leave that to my inner critic.* Instead, she thought how nice it would be to cook for somebody. Well, not *for* somebody, exactly, but to share a meal with them. Of course, there were occasions when she ate her ham salad sandwich or her Friday splurge of crayfish and rocket pasta in the same room as Raphael read his newspaper, but that wasn't precisely what she had in mind. *In any case*, she thought with a wry smile, moving the pan's contents around with a spatula, *given that Raphael can speak fluent Italian, I doubt he'd be impressed by my carbonara.*

Would Carl be?

The pan sizzled unexpectedly and Jemma took it off the heat before anything bad happened. Maybe she should open the window. The kitchen was rather warm. She sipped her squash, leaning against the worktop.

No point thinking about that, said the smug little voice which Jemma had really hoped was finished for the day. *You were so busy running round after the customers and barking orders at him that I doubt he thinks of you in that way at all.*

'Thanks for your feedback,' said Jemma, and looked

29

longingly at the wine.

Then again… If we did have another member of staff – a new member of staff – then I'd be senior. Of course I would. Jemma's mouth dropped open. *Why didn't I think of this before? Here was I, thinking I'd failed, and actually the shop has grown to the point where we need to expand! It's twice as big, it makes a lot more money, and we need staff!* 'Hah!' She executed an overhand stroke with her spatula and smashed the irritating little voice in mid-air. 'Take that, self-doubt!'

The spaghetti carbonara which emerged at the end of the cooking process perhaps wasn't the best ever, since Jemma had had to rouse herself several times from dreams of saying to the faceless new assistant, 'Would you mind fetching five boxes of books from the stockroom and shelving them for me, please?', 'Could you mind the till upstairs while Raphael is out?', and her personal favourite, 'Do you think it's time for a cup of tea?' But what she had made was creamy, cheesy, and satisfying, even if the spaghetti had stuck together a bit, and she ate it at her little table without regret, accompanied by a glass of wine.

When her bowl was clean she looked at the second half of the bottle. She deserved another glass, certainly.

Must keep a clear head, she thought, screwing the top on and taking the bottle through to the fridge. *Work to do.* She pulled out the sofa-bed in anticipation, fetched her laptop and put it on the table, and made herself a strong coffee.

***

The next morning, Jemma was at the shop for eight

o'clock sharp. She had stock to move, tills to manage, and most importantly, Raphael to convince.

'Morning!' she called, as she let herself in. She hadn't expected a response, and was surprised when Raphael wandered into the back room a few minutes later, pyjama-clad and bleary-eyed.

'I thought it was my turn to open up,' he murmured.

'It is,' said Jemma. 'Tea?'

Raphael nodded. 'You seem very . . . cheerful,' he ventured, after a minute or so.

'I suppose I am,' said Jemma. 'I was thinking of what you said yesterday, about getting more help in the shop, and you're right.'

Raphael stared at her. 'Oh.' Another pause. 'So you . . . agree?'

'Yes, I do,' said Jemma, getting the best china from the cupboard. 'Now that the shop is so much bigger and more profitable, it's absolutely right that we expand. I'll be able to manage the new person just fine.'

Raphael squeezed his eyes shut, rubbed the right one, then looked at her as if it would help him to see her better. 'Did you say manage?'

'Well, yes,' said Jemma. 'I mean, I'll be senior, obviously, and if you're out hunting down books a lot of the time, then someone should have oversight of the shop. And it makes sense that that person should be me.' The kettle boiled, and she warmed the pot. 'I worked out an appropriate division of duties last night, and drew up a sample job description and person specification. Oh, and I drafted an advert.'

31

'An advert,' Raphael repeated faintly, like an echo that had grown bored with its job.

'Yes, of course,' said Jemma. 'Obviously we'll aim to attract a wide range of suitable applicants, then cherry-pick the best ones to invite for interview. I mean, we wouldn't want to employ just anyone who walks in off the street.'

'Wouldn't we?' Raphael asked with a sly grin, and Jemma remembered belatedly that she herself had done just that not so long ago.

'That was different,' she said. 'Anyway, I was qualified.' *I was*, she told herself. *Wasn't I?*

'I never said you weren't,' said Raphael. 'But don't you think this is all a bit much? I mean, I've found plenty of good assistants by sticking a notice on the door.'

'I bet you've had some stinkers, too,' retorted Jemma, throwing teabags into the pot and drowning them. 'Didn't you say that most of them didn't last a week?'

'True,' said Raphael, 'but that doesn't mean they were necessarily bad. Just – temporary.'

'I don't want temporary,' said Jemma. 'I want committed, and conscientious, and – and—'

'Comatose? Canonical? Cantankerous?' Raphael laughed. 'I'm sorry, Jemma, but you take these things so seriously that it's hard not to poke a bit of fun occasionally.' He assumed a contrite expression as she scowled at him. 'I'll take a look at your – stuff – and we'll agree an advert to go out in an appropriate publication. I shall also follow my usual procedure, and put the Help Wanted sign on the door. I've still got it in a drawer somewhere. Between us, I'm sure we'll find someone suitable.'

Jemma drew herself up. She wasn't about to let herself be outsmarted by a man in green paisley pyjamas. 'I'm sure we shall,' she said, and picked up the teapot. The tea was perhaps a little stronger than her preference, but that was what milk was for. 'Here's to our new assistant,' she said, raising her cup. 'Cheers.'

'Yes, indeed. Cheers,' said Raphael, and they clinked cups. And that, as far as Jemma was concerned, was that.

Chapter 5

'We did say a quarter past five, didn't we?' Jemma glanced at her watch yet again, then at the door.

'We did,' said Raphael. 'At least, I assume you did.'

It was interview day for the new bookshop assistant, and so far, it wasn't going exactly to plan. Jemma had managed to get tomato sauce on her top, thanks to an incautious bite into a fortifying bacon roll earlier, and had had to nip out and find a substitute. In the end she had bought a nice blouse from a local charity shop, but when she put it on, it was a fraction too tight and too short. She had been wriggling all afternoon. And now their first candidate was late.

Jemma had written a lovely advert, packed with keywords and phrases which ought to attract any aspiring bookshop assistant. Then she checked the rate per word in the local paper, and had to draw a line through it and start again. She had wanted to place an ad in a prestigious booksellers' publication, but Raphael managed to convince her that people looking for a job at that salary probably weren't scouring its glossy pages. Applications trickled in over the week: some typed (although the ones in Comic Sans or Papyrus went straight in the bin), some handwritten (ditto any written in green or violet ink). They ranged from the frighteningly professional to the frankly delusional. In the end they were left with three applications. The first demonstrated a lack of experience but a great deal of enthusiasm; the second Jemma almost wished she had written herself, so accomplished was the applicant, and the third was short, to the point, and ticked all the boxes. Jemma had high hopes of the second; but she felt it only fair to give the other two a chance.

Raphael cupped a hand to his ear. 'Did I hear a knock?' They both strained their ears and sure enough, Jemma detected a gentle but persistent tapping. 'Hopefully that's our first interviewee,' she said, going to the door.

She opened it to reveal a breathless, flustered young woman in the act of buttoning her jacket. 'Oh, hello,' she said, 'I do hope I'm not too late. I got lost, you see. I went the wrong way. On the tube.'

'That's quite all right,' said Jemma, though she felt that it wasn't. Knowing where one was going was the first rule of a successful interview. 'Do come in – is it Dora?'

'Yes, that's right,' said Dora, looking worried.

Jemma admitted her to the bookshop and introduced her to Raphael, who seemed to unnerve her even more. After Jemma had performed the preliminaries of enquiring about her journey, getting her a glass of water, and taking her downstairs, Dora perched on the edge of one of the armchairs Jemma had arranged to make things less formal, gripping it as if it might turn into a fairground ride at any moment.

'So, Dora,' said Jemma, smiling at her encouragingly, 'why would you like to come and work for us?'

Dora appeared stricken. 'Well, I like . . . I like . . . books?'

Jemma and Raphael tried to ease her along as best they could, but Dora was only too willing to talk about her lack of experience working in a shop, admitted freely that she had trouble adding numbers up in her head, and said firmly that she hated confrontation or unpleasantness of any kind. Knowing the bookshop and Folio as she did, Jemma decided that it would be kinder not to consider her. So she ended the interview as quickly as she could, and presently Dora was on her way. Where she would end up was anyone's guess.

Raphael sighed and stretched his legs out once the door had closed behind her. 'On the bright side,' he said, 'we have time for a cup of tea before our next arrival.'

But he was mistaken. No sooner had Jemma poured out than they heard three no-nonsense knocks on the door. 'He's early,' said Jemma. 'Darn.'

On the doorstep stood a well-groomed young man in a dark suit and conservative tie. 'You must be Jemma,' he said, extending a hand. 'I'm Marcus. Here for the job interview?'

'Oh yes, indeed,' said Jemma, feeling as if *she* was.

'You're a little early.'

'Yes, I am,' said Marcus. 'I always make a point of leaving extra time in case an unexpected event occurs. One never knows, does one?'

'No, one never does,' said Jemma, and stood aside to let him in.

Marcus refused a cup of tea, and merely asked for a glass for the water which he had brought with him. Within one minute he was sitting composedly in the armchair, a folder on his lap, waiting for Jemma and Raphael to get themselves organised.

Over the next half hour they were treated to a potted history of Marcus's employment career, from working in his parents' bookshop as a teenager, through his degree and subsequent postgraduate work in business studies and library science, and ending triumphantly with his position as manager of the leading bookshop in Tamworth. He discoursed eloquently on different book-classification systems, the historical legacy from the collapse of the Net Book Agreement, the psychology of bookselling, and the importance of A/B testing one's window displays.

Jemma hated him. Particularly when he said he would be more than happy to deputise as manager if she were ever on leave or engaged in other business. He didn't seem to be saying it with any malign intent, but, as he himself had said, one never knows.

They managed to dispatch Marcus one minute before the next candidate was due to arrive. 'I do hope he's late,' said Jemma.

'Ah well, it probably doesn't matter now,' said Raphael.

'Marcus is quite a find.'

Jemma gaped at him. 'You have to be kidding me. Him? He'd have us tied in knots by the end of the first day.'

'Don't you think he'd be good in the bookshop?' said Raphael. 'I imagine we can both learn from him. He's so professional.'

'Are you saying that I'm not professional?' demanded Jemma.

'No, not at all,' said Raphael. 'That isn't what I meant. But you have to admit that he knows an awful lot.'

'Too much,' said Jemma darkly.

Raphael looked at her curiously. 'Do I detect a note of jealousy, Jemma James?'

'Of course not,' said Jemma. 'As if.' But she found herself hoping against hope that the final candidate would turn out to be the one.

A decisive, yet unintrusive knock sounded upon the door at exactly the appointed time. Jemma leapt up. 'I'll get it,' she said.

'I had a feeling you might,' said Raphael, and sniggered.

At first when Jemma opened the door she couldn't see anyone. Then a figure stepped out of the shadow of the shop next door, wearing a black suit, shirt and tie. 'Good evening,' she said. 'Are you here for the interview – oh, it's you!'

It was the pale young man whom Folio had attacked only a few days before.

'Good evening,' he said, smiling. 'Yes, I am.'

Jemma consulted a piece of paper. 'Luke Varney?'

'That's right.'

He settled himself, looking much more at home than he had on his previous visit to the shop, and refused a drink, saying that he had just had one. At first Jemma had her fingers crossed under her notepad, and willed him to provide half-reasonable answers to their questions. But after a tentative beginning, his confidence grew and Jemma relaxed. He liked books; he had read widely and could talk about his favourite authors and why he liked them; he was methodical; he had an A in GCSE Maths. And, wonderful to relate, he had worked in a secondhand bookshop before, and seemed in no doubt that his previous employer would give him a good reference. Jemma made sure to take down the name and contact details of his previous employer. If she had her way, she would be sending them an email as soon as they had shown Luke out.

'Do you have any questions for us?' she enquired, leaning forward in her chair and remembering just in time not to smile too broadly in case she frightened him.

Luke considered. 'Let me think. You've outlined the salary and the benefits, you've talked about the possibility of overtime... Oh, there were a couple of things.'

'Oh yes?' enquired Raphael.

'Yes, about the overtime,' said Luke. 'If possible, could I do any extra work in the evenings? It's a bit difficult for me to get here before eight thirty in the morning. I don't mind working late, not at all.'

'I don't think that would be a problem,' said Jemma. 'To be honest, it would be good to have someone around in the evenings to help with cashing up. And if we do start doing events, that would work really well. Wouldn't it, Raphael?'

'It would,' said Raphael. 'Was there anything else?'

'Just – if you don't mind, I'd prefer to work in the fiction section.' Luke waved a hand at the shelves. 'Certainly at first.' Then he looked a little embarrassed. 'As I mostly read fiction, I feel I'd be best placed to advise people there.'

'That seems reasonable,' said Raphael. 'What do you think, Jemma?'

Jemma thought for a moment. She much preferred working downstairs. Partly because, like Luke, she felt more knowledgeable about novels than non-fiction; but also because she liked being able to chat to Carl and sneak a cheeky cappuccino when it was quiet. Then again, if the alternative was Marcus, she was prepared to make allowances.

'I'm sure we can work something out,' she said. It didn't have to be for ever. Part of Luke's training could involve familiarising himself with the various types of books upstairs, and then everything would be back the way she wanted it.

'Oh yes, and one more thing,' said Raphael. 'Will you be able to get along with our cat, Folio? After all, you two didn't get off to a very good start.'

Luke swallowed. At that moment Folio chose to saunter into the room. He looked at the luckless interviewee, then strolled to a position between Raphael and Jemma, sat down facing Luke, and stared at him.

'I'm sure we'll manage just fine,' said Luke. 'I shouldn't have attempted to stroke him when the shop was so busy. I'll wait until he makes a move towards friendship before I attempt it again.'

'Very wise,' said Raphael. 'Now, we have your telephone number and there isn't anything else I need to ask. You'll hear from us soon, either way.'

'Thank you for the opportunity,' said Luke, with a nervous smile. 'I do hope I can come and work with you.' He shook hands with them both – Jemma noticed the Mr Bump plaster had disappeared – and left without further ado. He had already vanished into the darkening street by the time Jemma closed the front door.

'Kettle on,' said Raphael. 'Decision time.'

'There is no doubt in my mind,' said Jemma. 'Luke all the way. I suspect training Dora to become a competent employee would be a full-time job. As for Marcus, I couldn't bear him for more than a day. He's so annoying, with his suit, and his folder, and those little nuggets of information about Dewey Decimal versus whatever the other one was.'

Raphael laughed. 'He'd do very well,' he said. 'But if I did hire him, I'd have to find myself a new bookshop manager within days. Or possibly break you out of jail.'

'I'm not murderous,' said Jemma. 'He just rubs me up the wrong way.'

'I had observed,' said Raphael. 'All right, for the sake of a quiet life, neither of those two. What about Luke? Can you work with him?'

'I don't see why not,' said Jemma. 'He's polite, he

41

knows his stuff, he's qualified. And possibly most important of all, he won't tell me how to do my job, or try and swipe it from under my nose.'

'Most territorial of you,' said Raphael. 'Very well, subject to a decent reference and the customary checks, Luke it is.'

A sharp meow sounded from below, and he looked down in surprise. 'Are you expressing an opinion, Folio?'

'He's probably peckish,' said Jemma. 'Wasn't he supposed to be fed half an hour ago?'

'Good heavens, you're right,' said Raphael. 'I'll do that now, and make a pot of tea, if you phone Luke and tell him the good news. Knowing you, you'll email his previous employer too.'

'Might do,' said Jemma, grinning. 'Although we've still got to cash up this afternoon's takings. To be honest, I'd rather email from my laptop. Typing on the phone is so fiddly.'

Raphael nodded in agreement, though Jemma was fairly sure that he had never done such a thing, and disappeared, followed by an eager Folio.

Jemma retrieved her phone from her bag and typed in Luke's number. It went to voicemail after a couple of rings. *He probably hasn't taken it off silent mode*, she thought, and left him a brief positive message asking him to return her call at his earliest convenience. *There*. Things were in motion, and she, for one, was pleased with the way it had all worked out.

'You're absolutely sure you can manage?' asked Raphael, for perhaps the third time.

'Yes,' said Jemma, again. 'All I'm doing is showing Luke the ropes, then setting him to do some easy stuff. If that's too much for him, we can always close the downstairs till and I'll keep him with me. Monday mornings are generally fairly quiet, anyway.'

'I know,' said Raphael. 'That's why I agreed to go and view this book collection.' He glanced at Jemma. 'I could still cancel it—'

'There's really no need,' said Jemma.

'No,' said Raphael. 'And we do need more books.'

They certainly did. While the few days following the opening had been considerably less hectic, they were still ploughing through their book stock at an alarming rate. 'What would happen,' Jemma said one evening, as they stood together and gazed at the depleted shelves, 'if we ran out of stock altogether?'

'That will never happen,' said Raphael.

'It could,' said Jemma. 'If we have a very busy day.'

Raphael shook his head. 'Even then, it wouldn't.' And he seemed so certain of the fact that Jemma felt pushing the matter further would be rude.

'Ah,' Raphael said, as a tap on the door was followed by its tentative opening and Luke's dead-white face in the gap. 'The man himself.'

'Good morning,' said Luke, although he didn't look as if it was. If anything, he looked as if he might be sick.

'Are you all right?' said Jemma. He wore sunglasses, and she imagined his eyes behind them, bleary and red-rimmed.

Luke swallowed. 'Yes, fine.' He managed a weak smile. 'I'm not a morning person. But I'm sure I'll get used to it in a day or two.'

'Of course you will,' said Jemma. 'Good thing you're a little early; Raphael will have time to say goodbye before he leaves.' She shot Raphael a significant glance.

'Yes, I'm off to acquire books,' said Raphael, holding up a set of keys. 'My carriage awaits. I should be back sometime after lunch.'

'Wow,' said Luke. 'Are you travelling a long way?'

Jemma snorted. 'I believe he is venturing as far south as Bromley,' she said. 'But I suspect lunch, and possibly elevenses, will form a key part of the expedition.'

'You know me so well,' said Raphael, and strode to the door.

He was arrested before he reached it by a querulous meow, as Folio galloped through the shop and skidded to a halt on the parquet floor beside him.

'I wondered where you'd got to,' said Raphael, stroking his head.

Folio meowed again, then rubbed his cheek against Raphael's hand. 'Marking your territory, eh?' Raphael chuckled. 'Back soon, Folio.'

Folio jumped into the window display and watched as Raphael passed out of sight.

'And he's off,' said Jemma, putting the latch on the door. 'Now, we don't open until nine o'clock, and I'm not expecting Carl till at least then, as the café opens at nine thirty, so it's the perfect opportunity to show you around the shop.' She glanced at Luke, who was still wearing his sunglasses and a heavy coat. 'Are you absolutely sure you're all right? Would you like a cup of tea?'

Was she imagining it, or did Luke shudder? 'No, thanks,' he said. 'I don't – that is, caffeine has a bad effect on me, so I tend to stay away from it.' He rummaged in his black rucksack and brought out an enamelled metal drinks bottle. 'I'll stick to this.'

'OK,' said Jemma. 'Mind if I make myself one?'

'No, go ahead,' said Luke.

Mug in hand, Jemma began the tour. 'As you'll be downstairs mostly – at least at first – we won't spend too long in the main shop,' she said. She demonstrated the workings of the till, enquired whether he knew how the card reader worked (he did), and pointed out the various categories of books. 'Right, let's head to the stockroom.'

On the way, she indicated the cupboard under the sink. 'You'll find anything you need in there. First-aid kit, cleaning materials, household stuff in general. That sort of thing. I'm sure you can work out the fridge and the kettle.'

She opened the door to the stockroom, switched on the light, and ushered Luke in. 'As you can see, we're running a bit low at the moment, but hopefully Raphael will fix that this morning.'

'There must still be an awful lot of books,' said Luke, going halfway down the middle aisle and revolving slowly. 'How do you keep track of them all?'

'We don't,' said Jemma. She caught sight of Luke's horrified expression, and her grin disappeared.

'What do you mean?' he asked, looking very serious.

'Oh, well, obviously we've got a broad idea of what goes where,' Jemma gabbled. 'But given all the books passing through, it would be counterproductive to maintain detailed records when a book could come in and go out on the same day.'

Luke took off his sunglasses, as if to see her more clearly. 'So how do I find anything?'

Jemma smiled in what she hoped was a reassuring manner. 'You probably won't at first, but Raphael and I can direct you.'

'Oh, all right.' He wandered further down the aisle, trailing his hand along the shelf, and Jemma exhaled slowly.

Crisis averted. She had been so looking forward to having an extra pair of hands in the shop that she hadn't given any consideration to how she would explain away its peculiarities. And to be honest, the shop was almost all peculiarities. *We'll have to muddle on for now*, she thought. *When Luke's been here a while, it will probably seem quite normal.*

She composed her face as he came towards her. 'Have you considered labelling the shelves?'

'I suppose we could,' said Jemma. 'But at the moment we don't have time for any extra work. Just getting the books on the shelves and selling them is about all we can do. Oh, and posting on social media when we remember.'

Jemma had felt rather aggrieved when she realised at the end of the grand reopening day that she had not had time to take photos or update the shop's status. In the end she had had to compose a quick post when she got home, and illustrate it with a stock photo of books. Now, that would change. 'Are you good with social media?' she asked.

'Not bad,' said Luke cautiously. 'I tend to interact in closed groups, mostly.'

'But you could take a photo every so often, and write a post, and maybe add a hashtag or two?' she persisted.

Luke looked relieved. 'Oh yes, I could do that.'

'Excellent.' *Delegation accomplished,* thought Jemma. 'Let's head downstairs.'

'So when did you discover this?' asked Luke, as they gazed around the huge, silent lower floor.

'Just a few months ago,' said Jemma. 'We found stuff on the internet which suggested there might be something down here, and when we investigated, there was!'

'It's incredible,' said Luke, craning his neck and staring

at the ceiling. 'Would you mind if I took a look round? I mean, obviously I saw some of it when I came for the opening, but – it was busy, and I didn't know I would be working here.'

'Of course,' said Jemma. 'Go right ahead.' She leaned on the counter and watched Luke wander round. He pulled out a notebook, and seemed to be drawing himself a little map of the different sections. *Sensible and methodical*, thought Jemma. *Just what I want.*

'So everything is arranged by section, then alphabetically by author surname?' he asked.

'Everything except the children's picture books,' said Jemma. 'Those get picked up and put back so many times that we've given up keeping them in order.'

He laughed. Already he looked happier, and a bit less unhealthy. *I do hope he stays.*

Luke returned to the counter, pressed a button on the till, and the drawer opened with a ping. 'Is Mr Burns out of the shop often?'

'Call him Raphael; I do. And it depends,' said Jemma. 'He hasn't been able to get out much since the opening, because of all the customers. But now there are two of us I suspect he'll be out and about more. Even when he's in, he disappears to Rolando's fairly often in search of coffee and pastry.'

Luke's eyes widened. 'But you have a café.'

'Raphael claims that the coffee in the main shop tastes slightly different,' said Jemma, straight-faced.

'I see,' said Luke gravely. 'So he isn't hands-on, then?'

Jemma laughed. 'Well, he owns the shop, so he has

final say on everything, of course. But I run the place, mostly. With help from Folio, of course. And Carl providing the refreshments.' She studied Luke. 'So a lot of the time you'll be down here in charge of the fiction section while Carl runs the café, and I'll be upstairs in non-fiction.'

'Oh, OK,' said Luke. 'So in bookshop terms, it's just you and me.'

'Yes,' said Jemma. 'Just you and me. Is that all right with you?'

She wondered if she had perhaps stressed the responsibility of the job a little too early, but Luke seemed unfazed.

'Yes,' he said, running his hand along the shop counter as if he were stroking Folio. 'That's absolutely fine.' He took his coat off, hung it on the row of pegs by the customer toilets, and came back rolling up his sleeves. 'What do I have to do before we open?'

Jemma thought. 'Make sure the toilets are clean, check the float in the cash register, like I told you upstairs, and you're good to go. I'll bring down more stock, and then you're all set.'

'I guess I am.' Luke's brows knitted slightly with determination. 'I'll do my very best,' he said quietly.

'I know you will,' said Jemma. 'And if there's anything you can't handle, come and tell me.' But somehow, she suspected it wouldn't come to that. He might have looked ill at ease when he arrived in the shop, but now Luke appeared completely at home.

Chapter 7

It was Friday morning, half an hour before opening time. Luke had just arrived and was happily shelving books downstairs. Meanwhile, Jemma was pouring tea into two large mugs. Fridays tended to be busy, so this brew might have to last her until lunchtime.

'So what do you think?' asked Raphael.

Jemma looked as innocent as she could. 'About what?'

Raphael rolled his eyes. 'You know what. Today is Friday.'

'Is it?' said Jemma. 'Thanks for letting me know.'

'And you do know,' said Raphael, adding milk. 'It's the end of Luke's trial period today. What do you think?'

'I think he's great,' said Jemma. 'He comes in on time, he does what I need him to, the customers like him—' She grimaced. 'Sometimes they even ask for him.'

'Do they, now?' asked Raphael, smiling. 'How do you

feel about that?'

Jemma considered. 'All right, actually. I mean, it's good to have someone who knows what they're doing, and to feel that it doesn't all depend on me.'

Raphael raised his eyebrows.

'Don't look at me like that,' said Jemma. 'And he's organising the stock.'

One day, when the shop had just closed and they were alone together, Luke had sidled over and asked if he might have a word. 'Of course,' said Jemma, though his nervous expression alarmed her slightly. *What has he got in mind?*

Luke fidgeted with a pen on the counter. 'It's… I've been meaning to ask you pretty much since I came,' he said. 'It might not be appropriate, seeing as you're my boss…'

'Go on,' said Jemma, bracing herself.

'I wondered if we could, um, start scanning the books.'

Jemma stared. 'Scanning the books?'

'Yes,' said Luke. 'We don't know exactly what's where in the stockroom – well, I don't – but what we could do is scan the books when we put them out on the shelves, import the information into a database, then scan them again when we sell them. We'd be able to see what sells quickly, and over time, we'd get a much better idea of the stock in the shop.'

'Ooh, that's interesting,' said Jemma, forgetting her initial mild disappointment that Luke's question was related to books. 'Can we do that?'

'I don't see why not,' said Luke. 'I mean, it's easy enough to scan a book barcode with a mobile phone and get the data. The question is how we then move the data so that we can analyse it. Would you mind if I looked into it?'

'Not at all,' said Jemma. 'Fill your boots, in fact.'

And the experiment had begun. They had only been scanning books for two days, but already Luke was building up an impressive picture of what was selling in the bookshop, and what was going on the shelves. He had made graphs, and everything. Jemma gave Raphael a summary version of this information, resisting the temptation to batter him with bullet points. However, he didn't look as pleased as she had expected.

'I'm not sure I like the idea of all this – information gathering,' he said. 'What will you do with it all?'

'Analyse it,' said Jemma, unable to stop herself. 'Look at trends. Make forecasts. Plan.'

'I do wish you wouldn't use words like that,' said Raphael.

'What, *plan*?' said Jemma, grinning. 'I suppose it does have four letters.'

Raphael winced as he sipped his tea. 'Anyway, you're happy with him.'

'Yes,' said Jemma. 'He's exactly what the shop needs.'

Raphael studied her. 'You don't find him a little . . . quiet?'

Jemma considered the question. 'He does keep himself to himself,' she said. 'And I sometimes think it would do him good to get out of the shop at lunchtime, rather than eating on his own in the stockroom. Then again, better he does that than taking a long lunch or skiving off all the time. And his references were glowing.'

'True,' said Raphael. 'And it's hardly up to us to tell an employee how they should spend their lunch hour. Well, in that case I'll let Luke know he is a permanent fixture. Unless you want to do it?'

'I really don't mind,' said Jemma. 'To be honest, I'd rather you did. We have a visitor coming today, and I must make sure the shop is looking its best.'

'A visitor?' said Raphael, frowning. 'What sort of visitor?'

'A book blogger,' said Jemma. 'Now we've got time, we've been posting regularly on social media, and Stella sent me a message to ask if she could visit the bookshop today. You probably won't have heard of her, but she's very influential. Hopefully she'll feature us on her blog.'

Raphael looked mystified, but not hostile. 'Do you need me to be around? I was planning to go and see a man about some books—'

Jemma waved a dismissive hand. 'We'll be fine. You go and do what you do best.'

'All right then,' Raphael said, with a quizzical glance, 'I shall do that. But I'll go and speak to Luke first.' Mug in hand, he wandered downstairs.

Jemma went into the main shop and made her customary checks. The shelves were full of books. There was plenty of cash in the till, and the window display hadn't collapsed overnight. Yet something niggled her. What was it?

Is it me, she thought, *or was Raphael a bit doubtful about Luke?*

There's no reason for him to be, she argued. *Luke's*

good at his job, he's settled in well, and he's got over his nervousness. I don't see how we could have picked a better assistant.

She regarded the shop counter critically, and fetched a cloth and some polish. *What you mean, Jemma, is that you're worried about this blogger coming, and you're transferring that to Luke. Really, you'd do much better to take it out on the counter.*

She sighed, sprayed polish on, and began buffing.

***

'Wow,' said Stella, or Stella the Bookworm as she was more commonly known. 'It's incredible.' She revolved slowly, her eyes like saucers.

'It is rather nice, isn't it?' said Jemma, trying not to preen too obviously.

Stella had been due to arrive sometime between ten and eleven, but at a quarter to twelve, just as Jemma had given up hope, she saw a pink-haired woman outside the window and her heart leapt.

'Sorry I'm a bit late,' said Stella, as soon as she entered the shop. 'I got held up coming in, then I spotted some amazing things while I was walking over and I *had* to get pics.'

'That's quite all right,' said Jemma, wishing evil on the amazing things, and hoping the photos were underwhelming. 'It isn't as if we're going anywhere. I'll finish serving this customer, and then I'll take you downstairs and give you a tour.'

She dealt with her customer, then picked up the walkie-talkie which lay beside the cash register. 'Luke, can you come up? Stella has arrived. Over.'

Nothing. She glanced at Stella, who was meandering among the shelves and weaving round the other customers, occasionally stopping to read a book title.

'Luke, I need you upstairs. Over.'

The walkie-talkie crackled into life. 'It's really busy. Over.'

Jemma frowned at it. 'Don't worry, I can deal with that. But I do need you here now. Over.'

Two minutes later, Luke appeared. 'Is it a bit chilly down there?' Jemma asked, as he was wearing his big coat.

'I'm feeling the cold today,' he said. He blinked, then took his sunglasses from his coat pocket and put them on.

'Everything's in order,' said Jemma. 'I'll show you around, Stella, then you can have a bit of a wander about if you like. Stairs, or lift?'

'Oh, stairs please,' said Stella. She took several pictures with her phone as they descended. 'What an amazing door. It looks like the entry to a magic kingdom. Oh yes, that's good.' She opened an app on her phone, and said into it: '*The imposing oak door reminds me of the entrance to a magic kingdom, full stop. And in a way, comma, of course it is, full stop. A kingdom of books.*' She pressed a button and grinned at Jemma. 'I always find it helps to capture ideas as soon as I get them.'

'You really have a way with words,' said Jemma. She opened the door and waved Stella through. *Please be good*, she implored the shop, silently. *Just until Stella's gone.* And she followed Stella in, her fingers crossed behind her back.

Chapter 8

Jemma was aggrieved to find that the shop wasn't particularly busy for a Friday lunchtime. *What was Luke talking about?,* she thought crossly. However, from her point of view, it was much easier to escort Stella around a shop that wasn't packed full to the brim, and without fielding enquiries from several eager shoppers along the way. She fed Stella as many soundbites as she could, including the long history of the shop, the discovery of the original cathedral crypt, and the quantity and variety of books that they could offer. Stella said 'Wow' to most of these, and also recorded several of them on her phone, which gratified Jemma immensely.

She was just talking about their new book-scanning system when she heard a loud cough behind her. She turned to find Brian the antiquarian bookseller fixing her with a stern look as he rocked backwards and forwards on his heels. 'Any chance you can get hold of Raphael for me?' he asked.

'Do excuse me,' Jemma murmured to the blogger. 'I'm sorry, Brian, he's out at the moment.'

'Well, do you know when he'll be back? Your assistant had no idea, and sent me down here.' He gazed about him. 'So this is the new floor, eh? Bet this takes some running.'

'Yes, it does,' said Jemma. 'Raphael is out sourcing stock for it now.'

'Books by the yard, I expect,' said Brian. 'Pile 'em high, sell 'em cheap.' He laughed, and nudged Stella.

'Raphael chooses his stock with great care,' Jemma said, in her most withering tone. 'We are a general bookshop, and we stock a wide range of books.'

'Excuse me?' Jemma felt a light touch on her arm. A tense woman was at her elbow, clutching a large handbag. 'I do wonder if you can help. I'm looking for Agatha Christie, and I can't find her at all.'

'We definitely have some,' said Jemma. 'She'll be in the Crime section.'

'Oh,' said the woman. 'I might have been in the wrong place. Could you tell me where the Crime section is?'

'Yes, it's over there.' Jemma pointed and the woman peered.

'I can't see, with all the people,' she said. Certainly they had acquired several more visitors in the last couple of minutes.

'OK, do you see that man in the blue T-shirt? If you go to where he is, then turn right, it's just down there.'

'Oh, I see.' She mulled this over for a few seconds. 'I'll

try, but I may have to come back.'

'So can you give me any idea of when Raphael might deign to return to the shop?' asked Brian.

'He didn't say,' said Jemma. 'So I suppose sometime today is the best I can offer you.'

He sighed heavily. 'I'll hang around for a few minutes. Take a look at what you've got. I'm sure he'll be interested to hear my opinion, if he ever returns.' He strolled towards General Fiction with a face like a thundercloud.

'Sorry about that,' Jemma said to Stella, who was taking it all in with an expression of extreme interest.

'You do have to do an awful lot, don't you?' Stella replied.

'Friday's a busy day, and lunch is a busy time.' Jemma glanced at Carl, who was dealing competently with a queue of customers. 'Our local café and deli, Rolando's, have opened a sort of junior branch, and it's very popular. I'll try and introduce you to Carl when the rush has died down.'

'Ooh, yes please,' said Stella.

'You can go back up now.' Luke, slightly breathless, arrived at her side.

She raised her eyebrows. 'Er, who's looking after upstairs?'

'Raphael's just got back,' said Luke. 'He's minding things. Although he did mention nipping out.'

'OK,' said Jemma, with what she felt was great forbearance. 'Would you mind the till? I want to make sure Stella has everything she needs.'

'Oh, don't you worry about me,' said Stella. 'I'm

always at home in a bookshop.' She jabbed at her phone and intoned '*I'm always at home in a bookshop,*' then beamed at Jemma. 'Do you mind if I take photos?'

'Oh no, please do,' said Jemma, waving a hand around the shop. 'Would you like a drink? I'll see if I can jump the queue.'

'A milky coffee would be wonderful,' said Stella, already eyeing potential scenes to photograph.

'I'll see what I can do,' said Jemma, and sped off.

She ducked behind the café counter. 'Milky coffee, disposable cup, soon as you can,' she said, out of the side of her mouth.

Carl made a face. 'There's a queue for a reason.'

'Just this once. Please?'

The corner of his mouth curled up. 'All right, seeing as it's you.' He made the coffee quickly and efficiently and fitted the lid on. 'Freebie?'

'I'll settle up with you later,' said Jemma. She took the cup and headed into the bookshelves, looking for Stella.

It was surprising how easy it was to lose sight of a pink-haired woman. *Where did she go?* thought Jemma, cruising among the shelves, cup in hand.

'Excuse me?' The Agatha Christie hunter appeared in front of her holding two books, with a slightly forced smile on her face.

'Oh good, you found them!' said Jemma.

'Yes, I did,' said the woman. 'But they weren't where they should have been. I did find the Crime section, but these books were in Science Fiction and Fantasy. That doesn't seem right at all.'

'No, it doesn't,' said Jemma. 'Why don't you take them to the till and let our assistant know.'

'Yes… Rather odd, don't you think?' The woman stood for a couple of seconds, meditating the oddness of it, then as if she had resolved an inner battle, made for the till.

As Jemma watched her go, her eye was caught by a flash of pink at the shelves near the till, and she set off in hot pursuit. 'Here's your coffee,' she said, handing it over.

'Oh, thank you,' said Stella, taking the top off and sipping. 'Lovely.' She put it on the shop counter, took a couple of steps back, and focused her phone. 'Say cheese!' she called.

Luke looked up just as the flash went off. His neutral expression transformed into a mask of terror, and with a yell, he flung himself behind the counter. The customer he was serving recoiled in horror, and her flailing arm knocked the coffee cup onto the floor.

'Oh, sorry,' called Stella. 'Did I startle you?' She hurried up to the counter and peered over it. 'Are you all right down there?'

Slowly, Luke's head, then his top half came into view. 'A warning would have been nice,' he snapped.

'Luke!' cried Jemma. Then she regretted her cross tone, for as well as looking furious he was deathly pale, and his hands trembled. 'Go and have your lunch break,' she said. 'I'll take over.'

'Sorry,' Luke mumbled in Stella's direction, and walked slowly away, brushing himself down as he went.

Jemma heard a rumbling laugh behind her, and turned to see Brian, arms folded, chuckling. 'Bit camera-shy, is he?' he asked.

'Just a bit surprised,' said Jemma. 'And Raphael's back, so if you'd still like a word, now's the time.'

He strolled off, his shoulders shaking with mirth.

'I'm so sorry about that, Stella,' she said. 'Did you get the shot you wanted?'

'Yes, I did,' said Stella. 'I might take another one with you, if that's all right.'

'Oh yes, that's absolutely fine,' said Jemma, and plastered a cheery smile on her face.

'Marvellous,' said Stella. 'I'll take a few more of the shop and the shelves. Don't worry about the coffee.' She nodded at the floor, where the coffee cup lay in a small puddle, then wandered off.

'Oh darn,' said Jemma. 'I'll get that cleared up.' She hurried off for equipment, mopped and dried the stone floor, disposed of the cup, then scurried back behind the counter. The Agatha Christie hunter was waiting patiently.

'I'd like to buy these, please,' she said. 'And the lady over there said I should tell you that I found them in the Science Fiction and Fantasy section.'

Jemma raised an eyebrow. 'I see. I'll make sure I let her know that you told me. That will be five pounds, please.'

The woman gave her a five-pound note. 'Thank you so much,' she said, taking the books, and tripped away with an air of having accomplished her mission.

Jemma sighed, then smiled at the next customer, who put three Terry Pratchett books on the counter. 'Should I tell you that I found these in Crime?' he said, grinning.

Jemma fixed him with a horrified stare. 'You didn't, did

you?'

'No!' he bellowed, and started laughing.

'Ha ha, very good,' said Jemma, and rang up the sale. But all the time she served the customers, her mind was whirring. *What's been going on down here? Why did Luke say the shop was busy when it wasn't? Did he mis-shelve the books, or has it happened some other way? And most importantly, why on earth did he react like that when Stella took a photo of him?* And not even the sale of the whole *Forsyte Saga* in one go could distract her from her thoughts.

A quarter of an hour later, Luke was back on the shop floor. 'I'll take over,' he said, not meeting Jemma's eyes. 'Sorry about earlier.'

Jemma studied him. He certainly looked better than he had when he left. The colour had returned to his face, and he stood taller, seemed more self-assured. 'If you're sure,' she said, stepping away from the counter.

'I'm sure,' he said, moving smoothly into place. 'Besides, Raphael probably wants a break.' He grinned, and Jemma grinned back before realising that Luke's smile was for the next customer, not for her.

She looked at Carl, who was still busy with his queue. 'OK, I'll go and see how Raphael's getting on,' she said to Luke's back, and headed upstairs.

She found Raphael sitting in the armchair, reading a book about paint effects and stencilling. 'Oh, hello,' he said. 'The rush is over up here.' He closed the book. 'If it's all right with you, I might—'

Jemma checked for customers, and saw none. 'Could I have a quick word?' she said. 'It's about Luke.'

Raphael eyed her. 'It doesn't look like a good word,' he observed.

'It's a worried word,' said Jemma. 'He's been a bit odd today.'

Raphael gave the book a regretful glance. 'In what respect?'

'Well, when Stella the blogger came he didn't want to come upstairs; he kept making excuses. Then he came down again as soon as you got back, and some books downstairs were mis-shelved, and when Stella took a photo of him he dived behind the counter and freaked a customer out.'

Raphael considered. 'Maybe he's a bit camera-shy.'

'That's what Brian said,' Jemma replied. 'What did he want, anyway?'

'He asked my advice about the restoration of a volume he's recently acquired,' said Raphael. 'But I reckon he fancied a snoop round the shop. He'd never admit that, of course.'

'Oh,' said Jemma. 'But what do you think about Luke?'

'I think he prefers working downstairs,' said Raphael. 'Putting books in the wrong place doesn't sound like him, though.'

'It doesn't,' said Jemma. 'I even wondered if he'd done it on purpose, but what would be the point?'

'Exactly,' said Raphael. 'I suspect the shop has

something to do with it. It doesn't always react well to new employees, as you know.'

Jemma recalled her own first week in the shop; the hazards that had appeared, the cobwebs that had materialised from nowhere, and the strange incident of the window display. 'I suppose you could be right,' she said.

Raphael laughed. 'I've spent enough time in the shop to know its little tricks. The other thing is—' He paused, as if thinking how to phrase his next sentence. 'The shop has been very busy lately. I mean, there's been fitting out downstairs, moving things round, and bringing new stock in. Add two new members of staff and it's not surprising that things are a little chaotic. And even if the shop were a little more like most shops—'

'You mean normal,' said Jemma.

Raphael winced. 'Everyone's normal is different, Jemma. Any shop would be bound to have a few mishaps if it suddenly doubled in size and had twice as many staff.' He eyed her. 'And you've been doing an awful lot, Jemma. When was the last time you had a proper lunch hour? Out of the shop, I mean; not just eating your sandwich or whatever, then getting back behind the till.'

Jemma thought. 'I have been eating properly,' she said, as a beginning.

'Yes, I've seen your quinoa salads and your apples and bananas,' said Raphael. 'But when was the last time you left the shop for a whole hour?'

Jemma didn't even need to think. 'About a month ago,' she said. 'The shop's been so busy, and you've had to go out and buy books, and there was the building work to oversee—'

'I'm not saying those aren't good reasons,' said Raphael. 'But today Luke is downstairs, I'm upstairs, and everything is in hand. So go and get whatever virtuous thing is in your lunchbox, buy yourself a treat to go with it, then take yourself out for an hour. I don't mind where you go, so long as you don't go sneaking into any other you-know-what shops to do research, or check out their displays, or look at the shelving arrangements. It'll do you good.' He paused. 'I don't want you to burn out. I do value you very highly, you know.' He nodded briskly. 'Now, be off with you.'

Jemma managed a smile, collected her quinoa and bean salad from the fridge, and unhooked her bag from the coat stand. 'See you in an hour then, I suppose,' she said, and headed for the door.

She had just reached it when Folio streaked into view and flung himself down in front of her. 'Oh, really,' she said, and bent to stroke him. Folio chirruped, and rolled onto his back for her to scratch his tummy. 'Where have you been all morning, anyway?' she said as she rubbed. 'I've hardly seen you.'

'Probably asleep, knowing him,' said Raphael. Folio gave him an indignant glare, then rolled onto his feet, lifted his chin for a last fuss from Jemma, strolled to the armchair and jumped on top of Raphael's book. Raphael sighed, scooped Folio up with one hand, and moved the book away. Folio sank into Raphael's lap and put his head on his paws.

Jemma laughed. 'I'll leave you two to it, then,' she said,

and left.

'Hello, stranger,' said Nafisa, as she pushed open the door of the mini-market. 'What can I interest you in today?'

'Chocolate,' said Jemma firmly. She could have had her pick of any number of tempting Italian pastries and desserts from Rolando's; but sometimes what you needed was a sugary chocolate bar filled with a flavour not found in nature. She selected a Peppermint Aero and a Diet Coke.

'Interesting combination,' observed Nafisa, ringing them up. 'How's the shop doing?'

'We're very busy,' said Jemma. 'That's why I haven't been in much. We've got a new downstairs, you see.'

'A new downstairs, eh?' said Nafisa. 'With more books?'

'Yes, and an extra Rolando's.'

'You *have* been busy,' said Nafisa. 'That throws my new pie display into the shade.' She indicated a cabinet next to the counter, where a selection of pastry items glistened beigely.

'I'll try one sometime,' said Jemma, 'but I've brought my lunch today.'

'Up to you,' said Nafisa. 'I'm vegetarian.'

Jemma strolled along Charing Cross Road feeling aimless. Perhaps Raphael was right. A great deal had changed in a fairly short time. Not just for the shop, but for her. All of a sudden she had a much bigger space to manage, not to mention two new staff, and Raphael was hardly ever there to help. *Not that Carl needs looking after, exactly*, she added hastily to herself. *He can manage*

67

himself perfectly well. But her vision of chatting to Carl in quiet moments, perhaps sharing a joke, or taking a coffee break together, had never materialised. Their breaks were never at the same time. And on the shop floor, one or the other of them was always too busy to talk. When the bookshop was beginning to quieten, at four o'clock or so, Carl was often still busy serving drinks. She sighed. *So much for getting to know him better.*

And then there was Luke, whom she had regarded as almost the perfect employee until about an hour ago. *Why did he dive behind the counter like that? If he didn't want Stella to photograph him, he could have blocked the shot with his hand.* She sighed. *But it probably was the shop playing tricks with the books,* she told herself. *Although it never did that with me.*

It couldn't afford to, she thought. *Remember how desperate things were when you first arrived? Fifty pounds on a good day? And you wondered how Raphael was going to pay you?*

She laughed at the magnitude of the change. Nowadays it wasn't unknown for Raphael to take money to the bank in thousand-pound instalments. If they could get a clear idea of what was in the stockroom, and set up the online shop she wanted, then it would become even more profitable...

Jemma's heart beat faster, and suddenly she felt rather breathless. She looked at her watch; forty minutes left of her hour. *Raphael's right,* she thought. *An hour to myself and I spend it thinking about the bookshop. I need to go somewhere quiet and zone out.*

Soho Square Gardens was nearby. She made her way there, sat on an unoccupied bench, admired the trees in their autumn clothes for a moment, then unpacked her lunch. She couldn't remember packing cutlery that morning, but sure enough, she had a spoon and fork wrapped in a paper towel. 'Autopilot,' she said, and winced. 'If you're not careful, Jemma, you'll grind yourself down like you did at—' She stopped before she got to the name of her last employer. 'And you don't want that,' she told herself severely. She unclipped the lid of her salad, opened the Diet Coke, and began her lunch.

If anything, I should work out how to slow things down, she thought, chewing. *I'll park the online shop idea, at least until we know how busy the actual shop will be. If we sell many more books, I'm not sure any will be left for the other bookshops.* She looked around guiltily at the mention of other bookshops, then remembered that as she wasn't in the bookshop, it didn't matter.

Then she recalled something Raphael had said months ago, when she was new and keen to get things moving. What had it been, exactly? Something about the shop having to balance with the other bookshops. *Would he explain what he meant if I asked him now? After all, I'm much more experienced.*

'He's had the bookshop for what, thirty years?' A teasing little voice laughed in her ear.

But I'm more experienced than I was, argued Jemma. *And I care about the bookshop, and I don't want to hurt it.*

She ate the last mouthful of quinoa, put her spoon and fork inside the box, and snapped the lid on. Time for

69

chocolate. She popped a segment into her mouth, closed her eyes, and leaned against the bench. Questions could wait until she got back. Some things were too important to rush, and a Peppermint Aero was one of them.

Chapter 10

Jemma returned to Burns Books feeling considerably calmer than she had done when she left. That said, as she approached the shop she felt a little frisson of nerves. Would everything be all right?

Raphael laughed as she pushed open the door. 'Nothing's happened,' he said, smiling. 'Apart from selling books, of course. You may find this hard to believe, Jemma, but there was a time when the shop had to manage without you.'

Jemma smiled back. 'I know,' she said. 'And you're right; I should ease up a bit.' She glanced around her. The upstairs of the shop, at least, was quiet. Even Folio had gone off somewhere. 'I was thinking about what you said,' she ventured. 'About keeping in balance with other bookshops.'

Raphael frowned. 'Did I? When?'

'Oh, ages ago,' said Jemma. 'When I first started, and I was trying to get you to let me do things in the shop. You talked about the shop's niche, remember?'

Raphael gazed at the books behind Jemma for inspiration. 'Oh yes, so I did. I'm afraid that was partly intended to calm you down a bit.' He grimaced. 'Sorry.'

'That's OK,' said Jemma, and reflected on how angry she would have been at the time, had she known that. 'You said *partly*. What was the rest?'

Raphael looked wary. 'I didn't want the shop to be too busy. You've seen now what can happen when it gets a little . . . over-excited.'

'I see,' said Jemma. And she waited. Perhaps she was mistaken, but she had a distinct feeling that there was something Raphael hadn't said.

Raphael shifted nervously in the armchair. 'I may nip out for a coffee in a minute—'

'How did the book buying go this morning?' asked Jemma. 'I did mean to ask, but somehow with everything else it slipped my mind.'

A casual observer would have said that Raphael's face remained impassive, but Jemma noted a slight furrowing of his brow. 'Quite well, thank you. A couple of rare books, and fifteen boxes of general stock.'

'Oh, like what?' asked Jemma. 'We could do with more science fiction; we had a run on Asimovs.'

'I'm afraid it's all still sitting in Gertrude,' said Raphael. 'I haven't had a chance to unload her yet.'

Jemma had originally imagined Raphael going on his book expeditions in a car either grand but dilapidated or completely impractical. When she was introduced to Gertrude, she had to bite her lip and turn away for a good few seconds. Gertrude was an ancient bright-orange VW camper van who looked as if she had escaped from a children's movie. She had a rakish air, as if she might at any moment come round the corner on two wheels, pursued by an old-style police car or the sleek, low-slung vehicle of a villain. Somehow being Raphael's book van seemed a placid retirement for her, and Jemma hoped that Gertrude had had a full and interesting former life.

'Well, if I mind the till up here and it's quiet downstairs,' she said, 'you and Luke could go and unload. Or maybe Carl could help, if the café is quiet. Three of you could get it done really quickly. Not that I'm saying I can't help unload the van, but—'

'But you're the manager, and I know what's in the boxes,' finished Raphael. He picked up the walkie-talkie and pressed the button. 'Raphael to Luke. What's it like down there? Over.'

A tinny reply came back. 'It's pretty quiet, two people at the till. Why, what's up?' A pause. 'Oh, over.'

Raphael chuckled. 'You young people, always expecting the worst,' he said to Jemma, and pressed the button again. 'Nothing's up, just wondered if you could help me unload some books.' He peered out of the window. 'If we hurry, we can get them in before it starts raining. Looks a bit dark outside. Over.'

'OK, coming up. Do you want Carl as well? The café's empty. Over.'

'Yes please,' replied Raphael, and put down the walkie-talkie. 'Operation Restock can commence,' he said, and wedged the front door open with the owl doorstop they kept for such occasions.

Luke and Carl arrived upstairs together. Luke peered outside, pulled his beanie hat from his coat pocket, and put it on.

'You probably won't be out long enough to get wet,' said Jemma.

Luke looked at the sky and pulled a face. 'You never know.' The three of them left, and Jemma took up position behind the counter in case a random customer walked in.

Boxes of books began to enter the premises a few minutes later, two at a time. 'How on earth can you see?' Jemma asked Luke, who carried his boxes high, with his forehead pressed against the top one.

Luke didn't answer, but took them through to the stockroom. When he returned, he seemed almost a different person. 'I've had a thought,' he said.

'I thought you might have,' said Jemma. 'What is it?'

'This is the first time that we've been able to bring books into a quiet shop,' said Luke. 'We could open the boxes and scan them right away.'

'Do what right away?' said Raphael, entering the shop weighed down by two more boxes.

'Scan the books,' said Jemma. 'For our stock database.'

'Oh,' said Raphael. He set the boxes on the counter. 'Right now, you mean?'

'There's no reason why not,' said Jemma. 'I mean, I could do it here—'

'Or I could,' said Luke. 'We could take the boxes to the

stockroom and I could scan them, and as I know exactly what we need downstairs, I could sort those ones into separate boxes and have them ready to take down.'

'Good heavens,' said Raphael. 'Very efficient.'

Luke picked up Raphael's boxes and walked through to the stockroom.

Carl arrived next, carrying three boxes and looking as if he had decided that was a bad idea at least a minute ago. 'Where do you want them?' he gasped out.

'Stockroom, please,' said Jemma, and watched him go, his shoulders back and his jaw clenched. She realised she was frowning. Yet she wasn't sure why, exactly.

Ten minutes later all the boxes were in, and Raphael disappeared to take Gertrude to her garage, wherever that was. 'I might go for that coffee on the way back,' he said. 'I feel as if I've been in the shop a very long time.'

'You have, for you,' said Jemma, and grinned. 'See you for cashing up.'

She leaned on the counter and doodled on the notepad. A flower, with two leaves at the bottom of its stem. A heart with an arrow through it. A pile of books. A sketch of a cat who might be Folio—

I haven't seen much of Folio lately, she thought. *I wonder where he's been. And I haven't seen him go downstairs, either.*

She shrugged. *He's probably out catching mice or birds, or something.*

But what's bugging me? She returned to the notepad. It wasn't the flower, that was for sure. The heart – well, she was too busy for that sort of thing. Although maybe that ought to change. *I should stop fretting whenever I'm at a loose end, and learn to enjoy it.* Her pen pointed to the pile of books. *That's it. I was going to scan them, but Luke cut in and took over. While he has a point, it still means that I'm stuck up here doing nothing, and no one's downstairs.*

Downstairs… Due to the current working arrangements, she hadn't been downstairs during a busy spell for about a week before this morning's adventure. *Was it different? And if so, how?*

Her brow furrowed in thought. It had been busy, though not as busy as it had on opening day. And the shop had misbehaved in a way that it had never done with her. The shop's tricks at her expense were generally designed to make her uncomfortable. But moving books into the wrong places was different. Could it be that the shop wanted to send customers away? But it was easy to move books back to the right places, and she doubted that any of their customers would worry over where books were shelved, so long as they could find them eventually. Browsing, after all, was one of the great pleasures of a bookshop.

The other option was that Luke had mis-shelved the books, either accidentally or deliberately. Again, it seemed unlikely. He was too careful, too meticulous.

Jemma sighed, and was on the point of drawing a line through the books when her pen stopped, and hovered above the paper.

What if – what if the shop wanted to get Luke into trouble?

But why? He seemed harmless enough. *He's a nice*

person, Jemma thought to herself. Then she remembered him on that first day, when Folio had scratched him. It had been a tiny wound, but still... Folio was much more placid these days, possibly because the shop was larger and tidier and he had more space to roam around. All the same, it was odd.

The stockroom door creaked, and she glanced up as Luke appeared. 'One for the shop so far, three on the shelves,' he said, smiling.

'How's it going?' Jemma asked, hoping that her thoughts weren't visible in her face.

'Fine,' said Luke. 'I feel as if I'm finally settling in, now I'm starting to sort things out in there.' He pushed his dark hair out of his eyes, and his smile broadened. He was still wearing his long coat, and appeared rather swashbuckling in his narrow jeans and big boots. Jemma found herself smiling back. 'I'd better get on with it. These books won't scan themselves.' He disappeared into the stockroom.

Jemma looked down at the notepad again. She drew a circle, added a dot in the centre, then drew the long and the short hand. *There's no way of knowing yet. I shall watch, and wait, and observe, and hopefully deduce.* On impulse, she went to the box in the back room and peeked inside. Edmund Crispin's *The Moving Toyshop* lay on top of the pile.

Trust you to pick a book I haven't read, she thought, and turned the book over to look at the blurb. Even then, she felt none the wiser.

Chapter 11

Jemma arrived on Monday morning equipped with a notebook and pen to record her observations. She'd even spent some time on Sunday debating precisely what to record. *Anything unusual* had been her first thought. Then she amended that to *Anything unusual for the bookshop.* But should she confine herself to things which definitely involved Luke, or should she record everything? In the end she decided that the latter would be the fairest course of action. After all, she couldn't be sure that Luke was the problem.

Monday passed without incident, and under that day's date Jemma could only write: *Nothing in particular. Must try harder*, she thought to herself. Then again, if there was nothing to observe and record, what was the point of inventing things? That would just be making work for herself, and creating a problem where none existed.

Tuesday started in much the same vein. When Jemma went downstairs for a final check before the shop opened, she found Luke adding to the float in the till. She took a quick tour around the shelves; nothing seemed out of place. Then she remembered that she hadn't mentioned the mis-shelved books to Luke. On Friday, the priority had been getting him away from the situation, then making sure the customer was dealt with appropriately. 'A customer reported some wrongly shelved books on Friday,' she said, keeping her voice light. 'She found Agatha Christies in Science Fiction.'

Luke frowned. 'That's odd,' he said. 'I'm pretty sure I wouldn't have put them there. Maybe one of the customers put them back in the wrong place.'

'Could be,' said Jemma. *Why didn't I think of that?* she asked herself. *That's obviously what must have happened!* 'I didn't think it was you,' she added.

'I hope I've got enough sense to know where the Agathas go,' Luke replied, and closed the till drawer with a snap. 'All ready.'

'Morning,' said Carl, shrugging off his coat as he walked in. 'Time to pick up the pastries from Big R.' He strolled towards the coat rack. To do so, he had to pass first Luke, then Jemma. And as he did so, he gave Jemma a significant look. She felt as if she were being prompted.

It was so hard not to stare back, or mouth anything. How should she respond? Already she could feel her face heating up. 'Need a hand?' she asked. She thought about adding a friendly grin, but suspected that if she tried it would come out wrong.

'Yeah, if you wouldn't mind,' said Carl. 'Rolando said they'd start sending a few more after we ran out yesterday.' Suddenly he drew himself up, assumed a haughty expression, and declared 'We must keep Little R well-fed and happy,' in a strong Italian accent.

Jemma laughed. 'So our café is Little R now?'

'I guess so,' said Carl, in his normal voice. 'Although at the rate we're going, we could be Medium-Sized R soon.'

'Maybe,' said Jemma. 'But we'd better get a move on if I'm going to be back for opening time. See you later, Luke,' she called, on her way to the door.

'What was that about?' she asked, once the door of the shop had closed behind them.

'Come on,' said Carl, and she had to hurry to keep up with him as he strode down the road to Rolando's. He pushed open the door and Jemma followed him in. The café was already busy, but two large lidded plastic boxes waited on the counter.

Giulia bustled out of the kitchen. 'Thirty extra today,' she said briskly. 'We see how it goes, yes?'

'Thank you,' said Jemma.

'Is nothing,' said Giulia, and with a quick bob of her head she disappeared again.

Carl glanced around them at the various customers enjoying their drinks and pastries. 'Come on,' he muttered, and walked towards the back of the café. Behind a plain wood door was a corridor, and he opened the first door on the left to reveal a small walk-in cupboard. 'In here.'

'Is this really necessary?' asked Jemma.

'Dunno,' said Carl. 'But I'd rather be too careful than

not careful enough.'

'Have you been reading spy novels on your break?' asked Jemma, with a smile.

'Something isn't right,' said Carl. He hesitated, a tentative expression on his face. 'This probably sounds weird, and I don't know what it is, but the shop feels – it feels *heavy*.'

Jemma stared at him. 'How do you mean?' she asked, though she had a fair idea of what he meant.

'You know how it feels when there are dark clouds overhead, and it isn't raining yet, but you know it's going to?'

Jemma's smile faded.

'I see you do,' he said. 'And it's felt like that downstairs pretty much since Luke started.'

'Really?' asked Jemma. 'I must admit, I haven't noticed. It was a bit strange on Friday, but I put that down to it being busy. And having Stella in, of course.'

'Ah,' said Carl. 'And it isn't like that upstairs?'

'No,' said Jemma. 'But it's never as busy.' She frowned. 'Are you absolutely sure?'

Carl moved closer, and lowered his voice. 'At first I thought I was imagining things,' he said. 'It felt odd the first day Luke was downstairs without you, but I thought that was because, well—' He looked down for a moment. 'Because I'm used to having you around.' A sudden, sheepish grin. 'But the feeling has been getting stronger. At first it was just in the back of my mind, like a niggle every so often, but after a couple of days I felt worried. When you or Raphael are downstairs, it goes away. It's only when

Luke's down there on his own. And yesterday I walked in after my break and it hit me as soon as I stepped through the door.' Jemma saw fear in his brown eyes. 'I thought about telling you then, but the shop was too busy, and Raphael was out.'

'Oh,' said Jemma. She felt as if Carl had handed her a huge responsibility, wriggly and bulky and awkwardly shaped, and she had absolutely no idea how to manage it. 'Um, why do you think you feel it, and Raphael and I don't?'

'Maybe it's to do with the acting,' said Carl. 'We're trained to feed off the audience's reaction, so you get sensitive to atmosphere. And I spend more time alone with Luke than either of you.'

'That makes sense,' said Jemma. But even as she said the words, she thought, *Is he over-reacting?* 'But what do we do? I can't dismiss Luke on the grounds that he makes you feel a bit funny.'

'I know,' said Carl, looking injured nevertheless. 'That's one of the reasons why I haven't said anything. That, and it being so hard to get a word with you alone.'

'OK,' said Jemma, though she didn't feel OK. She felt uncomfortable, and she wasn't sure whether it was because of what Carl was telling her, or the fact that they were crammed into a cupboard together, and she was very conscious of how close he was. She could smell his aftershave, and if she took a step closer— 'Well, um, if I give you my mobile number, we can text each other.' She pulled out her phone and showed him the number.

'We could,' said Carl. He took out his own phone and

typed her number into it, sent a text which said *Hi*, then pocketed it. 'I was thinking—' He gazed at his feet.

The pause lengthened, and Jemma checked her watch. 'It's five to nine—'

'We could meet up,' said Carl. 'Outside work, I mean. Somewhere we can't be overheard. We could meet up, and discuss what we've seen, and *felt*.'

Jemma looked into Carl's face, inches from hers. He seemed worried. Worried, and beneath that, upset and trying to hide it. 'You're serious about this, aren't you?'

A slow nod. 'Yes, I am. I don't know what it is, but I don't like it.'

'Then we must sort it out,' said Jemma, with the best brisk managerial air she could summon. 'Today's Tuesday. How is Thursday for you, after work?'

'I can do that,' said Carl. 'We could go to your place, if that's all right?' He gave her a tight little smile. 'Sorry to ask, but it isn't the kind of thing we can discuss in public. And if I take you to ours, you won't get a word in edgeways. Plus my mum would probably want to suss you out.'

'Uh-huh,' said Jemma, trying not to show her alarm. 'Let's say Thursday, and see how we go. We might have nothing to discuss, and in that case, we don't need to meet.'

'I'm not expecting you to cook,' said Carl. 'Or tidy up.'

'That's good, because I wasn't going to,' said Jemma. 'Now, let's get those pastries back to the bookshop before we get in trouble.' She opened the door, and as she did so Carl's expression transformed into a cheeky grin. He strolled out of the stockroom and high-fived one of the shop staff coming the other way, who raised his eyebrows at Jemma, then grinned back.

'Shall I take one of the trays?' she asked, as they approached the counter.

'No need,' said Carl, lifting them both easily. 'You can get the doors for me.'

Jemma looked at him curiously, but Carl appeared his normal happy, positive self, and it was hard to believe that the conversation they'd had moments ago had happened at all. She had a feeling that she wouldn't see any sign of worry on Carl's face again until they were tucked away from prying eyes.

Chapter 12

Jemma kept an eye on Luke that day, but it was not a close eye. While Raphael didn't have any book-buying trips scheduled, he was in and out a lot: nipping next door to Rolando's, taking a long lunch break, and going for a chat with two other bookshop owners in Charing Cross Road.

'Are you doing business with them?' Jemma asked.

'Business? Oh, not exactly,' said Raphael. 'More seeing the lie of the land.' And before Jemma could ask him exactly what that was supposed to mean, he left.

So it was down to Carl. Jemma listened out for her phone in case he texted. She even put it in her pocket, something she never usually did, but after an hour or two she replaced it in her bag. It was too distracting. Every time her phone buzzed her heart leapt, expecting the piece of damning evidence. However, it was always just another social-media notification.

The one exception to this was a notification that the bookshop had been tagged in a post by Stella the Bookworm. Jemma unlocked her phone with trembling hands, and clicked.

She needn't have worried. Stella had written a really nice piece, praising the bookshop's stock and its furnishings. She complimented the coffee which she had barely had a chance to drink. And mercifully, she didn't mention *the incident*. She even, at one point, referred to 'Jemma, the capable bookshop manager'. Jemma could feel her cheeks getting warm, and she couldn't stop herself from grinning. She shared the link on the shop's social-media feeds: *Thank you so much, Stella the Bookworm, for this lovely article about us! Come and visit us again any time!* She sighed out a breath, and only then realised how worried she had been that the shop would get a bad review, and they would be back as the second-worst bookshop in Britain again. Luke was, she felt, at least partly to blame for that.

She showed the post to Raphael on one of his brief returns to the shop. He read it, and as he did his expression resembled that of a proud father. 'That *is* good,' he said. 'Well done, the shop. And you, of course,' he added hastily.

Jemma rolled her eyes, but she was still smiling.

The only text from Carl that day came just after he had left. *Nothing particular to report but weird feeling still there.*

Jemma frowned at the message. What could she say in reply? In the end she settled for: *Fine upstairs. Thanks for watching out*. She hoped Carl didn't find her message dismissive. But what else could she say?

At the end of the day she left slightly after Luke, and as she walked to the station a vague sense of unease prickled at her. Was something going on? Was she perhaps not tuned in enough to the shop to feel it? Then again, Raphael didn't seem bothered, and it was his shop.

Once home, Jemma threw herself into cooking beef stroganoff to take her mind off things. But even as she ate, sitting at the little drop-leaf table, she looked at her flat through a stranger's eyes. The walls could do with a fresh coat of paint; the original pale yellow had lapsed into a sort of jaundiced cream. The curtains and the carpet didn't match. She hadn't folded up the sofa-bed properly, and it appeared lumpy and misshapen. *Not that I'll be inviting him to it*, she thought to herself. Then she almost spat out her mouthful of food. *Not like that!*

Then she sighed. As things were, it looked likely that they wouldn't need to meet on Thursday after all. *So you can stop worrying about that, Jemma*, she said aloud, and silenced herself with more food. But when she had finished dinner, she still went to the little corner cupboard where she kept her clothes, pulled out a casual, pretty floral dress, and checked it for creases before hanging it up, tutting at herself, and closing the door on it.

Wednesday was much the same. The shop was busy enough that Jemma didn't have time to worry about what might be going on downstairs. Indeed, Raphael actually stayed in the shop that afternoon, and Jemma took the opportunity to go downstairs and help in the Fiction section.

She found Luke in a cheerful mood, joking with the customers as he served them or answered their questions, and she felt a little pang of envy that she spent so much time upstairs. Then she told herself that it was her job to manage, not to be on the till all the time. In any case, she got her chance when Luke asked whether he could go and scan books in the stockroom. 'And I'll bring some more down,' he said. 'I labelled the boxes I scanned the other day, so it should be much easier to find stock. For me, at least.' He grinned.

'Yes, you do that,' said Jemma. 'I see our two Golden Age crime ladies are in, so I'll put a request in for that, as they usually buy a fair few between them.'

'Aye aye, Captain,' said Luke, and saluted. At least he wasn't wearing his big coat, in which case the gesture would have seemed more military. She noticed that instead of his usual black ensemble, his shirt was midnight blue.

'That suits you,' Jemma said. 'The shirt, I mean.'

A slow flush crept from Luke's neck to his face. 'Thank you,' he said. 'I'll go and sort out those books.'

Jemma turned her attention to the next customer. But she glanced towards the doorway just as Luke looked back, and their eyes met for a moment before he vanished behind the great oak door.

Now it was Jemma's turn to go a bit pink. She shot a guilty look in Carl's direction, but he was busy at the coffee machine. *In any case*, she thought, as she slipped Dodie Smith novels into a Burns Books bag, *I didn't mean anything like that. I just meant that the blue shirt suited him better than the black ones. It makes him look a bit less washed out.*

She rang up the purchases, and watched the customer count out their change. Working at the bookshop seemed to suit Luke. He definitely seemed less poorly and pale than he had when he arrived. And while he still ate his lunch in the stockroom, he occasionally accepted an offer of tea. He had even brought in some decaf teabags which sat in the kitchen, ignored by everyone else. Perhaps Raphael was right, and it was a matter of the shop and Luke getting used to each other.

And then came Thursday.

It began normally enough, with a journey in on a fairly busy tube train. Jemma couldn't get a seat, so hooked her elbow around the pole by the doors, and took the opportunity to text Carl: *If nothing happens today, we don't need to meet later.*

There was no reply. *He's probably travelling in too.* In any case, she would see him soon, for she was only a couple of stops from work now.

She was surprised to find the lights already on in the shop when she arrived, and Raphael putting his jacket on, accompanied by a volley of meows from Folio. She noted that he was wearing a suit and a coordinating shirt and tie, unlike his usual colourful mishmash of garments, and a stack of unassembled cardboard boxes leaned against the counter. 'Off on a book expedition?' she asked.

'I am,' said Raphael. 'Got a phone call at seven yesterday evening from the widow of Sir Tarquin Golightly.'

'Sir Tarquin Golightly, eh?' said Jemma.

'The very same,' said Raphael. 'Scientist, inventor, and renowned book collector. Lady Golightly, however, can't stand the "dusty old things", as she calls them, and has invited me to Hertfordshire to deal with the problem.' His eyes gleamed blue. 'Obviously I told her I would be more than happy to assist.'

'Do you know what sort of books he has?' asked Jemma.

'I've heard rumours,' said Raphael, rubbing his hands. 'Let's just say this sort of opportunity comes along once in a generation.'

Folio let out another meow, then flung himself on the parquet floor and wriggled at Raphael's feet.

'Stop moaning, Folio, you've had your salmon.' Raphael reached down and tickled his tummy. 'Be careful of him, Jemma, he's in a bit of a funny mood.'

'When do you think you'll be back?' asked Jemma. 'Hertfordshire's not that far away.'

'It isn't,' said Raphael. 'But there will be an awful lot of books to go through. And if Lady Golightly asks me to stay to lunch, then it would be most impolite of me to refuse.'

Jemma eyed his thin figure, and sighed. Given Raphael's enthusiastic consumption of pastries, fast food, and caffeinated beverages, he ought to have been the size of a house and permanently jittery.

'I won't ask what you're thinking,' said Raphael, with a smile. 'Your expression tells me that I don't want to know.'

Jemma grimaced. 'You're probably right,' she said,

opening the door. 'Good hunting.'

'The shelves await,' Raphael declared. He hefted his stack of flat boxes, and strode off.

Jemma sighed. That meant another day spent mostly upstairs. Then again, it probably didn't matter. Yesterday had been fine, and the day before, and Carl was more than capable of observing what went on.

Carl turned up, and went to get supplies from Rolando's. When he came back, Luke still hadn't arrived. 'Maybe he's having trouble getting in,' said Jemma. 'The tube was busy this morning. I'm not entirely sure where he's coming from, but there could be trouble on his line.'

'Could be,' said Carl. He glanced at her. 'I got your message.'

'What do you think?' asked Jemma. It felt odd to be talking normally in the empty shop. Almost as if they were doing something forbidden. She caught herself making sure no one was there.

Carl's face was expressionless. 'I don't know,' he said. 'Nothing's happened, but I still think…'

'You still think what?'

'I don't *know*,' he repeated. 'But I don't like it.' A pause. 'I'll go downstairs and get things ready.'

Nine o'clock came, and Luke did not. Jemma opened the shop and found three people waiting outside. 'We're a bit low on staff today,' she said as she ushered them in. 'So can you bring your books to the upstairs till, please.'

All three of them clattered downstairs. *Hurry up, Luke*, Jemma thought. She picked up the walkie-talkie, then remembered that Carl probably wouldn't answer it since it was really for bookshop staff. She fetched her phone, and texted: *Luke still not here, have told customers to use upstairs till. Any questions you can't handle, ask me. Sorry.*

A few more customers came, and a few more, and at nine thirty there was still no sign of Luke. *Should I phone him?* She hunted through the drawers under the counter for his number, but couldn't find it. *Perhaps he's ill.*

Even if he is, he should still ring in, her managerial voice nagged. *Or at least text. Everyone knows that's what you do. Or he could get someone to ring for him, if he's too ill.*

But did he have anyone? He'd never mentioned anybody. No partner, or friends, or family. *Anyway,* thought Jemma, *there's nothing I can do but get on with it.* So she got on with doing just that.

Except that there wasn't anything to get on with. The odd customer to serve, of course, but they trooped up obediently with their books, and they all had the right money and no weird questions. She nearly wished for a difficult customer to give her something to do. Then she recalled some of the customers she had dealt with, and thanked her lucky stars.

Jemma made herself a cup of tea at eleven, and even considered popping downstairs for a snack to go with it, but conscientiousness won out, and she stayed behind the counter. *When he gets here—* Then she decided she might as well sit in the armchair and read as it was so quiet, and soon, lost in Narnia, she forgot all about it.

She was so absorbed in her book that she barely

glanced up when the shop bell rang. When she did, she couldn't look away.

Chapter 13

Luke stood in the doorway, panting. He was as white as a corpse, his eyes bloodshot. His hand gripped the door as if he might collapse otherwise.

All thoughts of shouting at him disappeared. 'What on earth has happened?' Jemma asked. 'Here, sit down.' She sprang up and led him to the chair, but he resisted when she tried to push him into it.

'I'm late,' he said. 'Something, um, happened. But I'm here now.'

'Should you be here? You look terrible.'

A smile flickered for an instant on his pale lips. 'Thanks. I'm fine.' He took out his drink, swigged from it, then wiped his mouth on the back of his hand. 'I'll get myself downstairs.'

'Take the lift,' said Jemma. 'I'm worried about you.'

'I'm *fine*,' he muttered, and shuffled off, still in his long coat and beanie hat.

As soon as he had gone, Jemma picked up her phone and texted Carl. *He's arrived.* She didn't feel she needed to say any more. Carl would be able to work it out for himself when he saw Luke.

Two minutes later she got a reply. *What's he been doing? He looks dead.*

He didn't say, Jemma replied. *All OK down there?*

Quiet so far. Serving a lot of cappuccinos ;-)

Jemma's mouth twitched. *Save one for me ;-)* She replaced her phone in her bag. Maybe they *could* meet later, and go out for a drink and a chat. That would be nice. She'd wait a bit, maybe until after lunch so that she didn't seem too keen, then make the suggestion.

Then a customer came in who actually wanted a non-fiction book. Jemma was kept busy bringing books to the counter, only to be told that they were interesting, but not quite right. She succeeded on her tenth try. Then she remembered her wish earlier, and cursed herself.

More customers came, mostly for downstairs, but enough stayed upstairs to keep Jemma occupied. At least now she wouldn't have to deal with all the purchases. She hoped Luke was managing downstairs. *Then again*, she thought, *it isn't difficult. And if he's having problems, he knows he can send them up to me.*

As if on cue, a dapper elderly gentleman approached the counter. 'Excuse me,' he said, 'I'm looking for a book. It wasn't on the shelves downstairs, but the young chap on the till thought you might have a copy in stock.'

'We very well might,' said Jemma. 'What is it called?'

He adjusted his pocket square. '*Ulysses*. By James Joyce.'

Jemma bit back a retort that she knew who had written *Ulysses*, thank you very much, and said, 'If you wait a minute, I'll see what I can find in the stockroom.' *I'm sure we had one downstairs*, she thought, as she opened the stockroom door and switched on the light. *Then again, we might have sold it.* She gazed at the shelves. Luke had labelled the boxes nearest the door. None of those looked likely. 'Pot luck, then,' she said, taking a random box off the shelf and returning to the shop.

'I'll open this and see what's inside,' she said, reaching for the scissors. She cut the tape, and lifted up the flaps.

She lifted out the first book: *Lost Horizon*.

Underneath that was *Lost Empires*.

And beneath that, a guidebook for the Lost Gardens of Heligan.

Jemma lifted out book after book, feeling increasingly worried, but *Ulysses* was not there. 'I can try another box, if you like,' she faltered. In all the time she had worked at the bookshop, she had never failed to find a book that a customer wanted.

'Thanks, but I'm in a bit of a hurry,' said the elderly gentleman. 'I'll leave my number, then you can call me when you have it back in stock.' He wrote his name and number on the notepad, and printed ULYSSES BY JAMES JOYCE in neat square capitals. 'Good day to you,' he said, and went out.

Then another customer came forward. 'Have you got a copy of *Whose Body?* It's by Dorothy L Sayers. I looked downstairs, but it wasn't there, and the lad on the till said —'

'I'll try the stockroom,' said Jemma, grimly. She pulled out another box, opened it, saw that the book on top was *Gone Girl*, and shivered. Dutifully, she went through the rest of the box, but had no luck. 'If you leave your name and number, we'll call you when we have it in,' she said, presenting a fresh sheet of the notepad.

Two more unfulfilled queries later, she grabbed the walkie-talkie. 'Jemma to Luke. Please don't send more customers up for books. If they're not on the shelves, I can't help. Over.'

She expected a snarky reply along the lines of: *If you scanned the books when they came in then it wouldn't be a problem.* Instead, Luke's voice sounded exhausted through the crackling. 'Sorry, I didn't know what else to do. Over.'

Jemma sighed. When she had dispensed with the queue, she went to fetch her phone. *Looks like tonight's meeting is back on,* she thought. *I knew I should have hoovered before I left.*

Her phone screen was full of messages from Carl. The one at the bottom, the first that he had sent, read: *The air is really heavy.* The next: *It's like the air is fizzing.* And finally: *You have to come down, Jemma. Please reply, and I'll come and mind upstairs.*

That message had been sent two minutes before. Jemma pressed *Reply. OK.*

Carl arrived thirty seconds later, and Jemma was shocked at his pallor; his skin had an odd greyish tinge. 'It's not that I'm scared,' he said, as soon as he saw her.

'Well, I am, I guess, but *I* can't do anything about it. I'm hoping the shop will calm itself if you go downstairs.'

Jemma felt the blood drain from her face. 'What's going on?'

Carl shook his head. 'No idea. I felt this chill, and when I looked at Luke he was staring at his phone. Then customers started going up to him and saying they couldn't find the book they wanted, and that the books were in the wrong place, and someone tripped over Folio—'

'Oh heck,' said Jemma. 'Are they all right?'

'Yes, but not best pleased,' said Carl. 'I apologised, and sat them down in a chair with a free drink. And then a light bulb blew.'

'Oh no,' said Jemma.

'And there was a rumble—'

But Jemma was already on her way. As she rushed through the back room she saw Folio standing in front of the stockroom door. He hissed at her, his tail fluffed out with rage. 'No need to do that at me,' she muttered, and ran down the steps.

She heard raised voices, and braced herself as she opened the great oak door. Then she stared at the scene before her.

Close by, two customers were tugging the same book in different directions. Several more customers surrounded Luke at the till, all talking at once. A woman in a tie-dye skirt was standing behind them, saying plaintively to no one in particular, 'I just want to be served, that's all I ask.'

Jemma dashed up to her and took the book gently from her hand. 'I'm so sorry for your wait,' she said. 'That will be two pounds, please. Don't worry, I'll ring it up for you, if you don't need a receipt.'

The woman brightened, and pulled a small purse from her bag. 'Thank you ever so much,' she said. She took the book, put it carefully into her bag, and wandered off.

'Excuse me please,' called Jemma, and moved people aside to get to the till, where she deposited the two-pound coin. 'We can only serve two people at a time, because there are only two of us. Who's next, please?'

Everyone spoke at once, angry expressions on their faces, and Jemma couldn't make any sense of it at all. 'Please, one at a time!' She raised her hands for silence, and didn't get it.

Then the lights went out.

A huge, collective gasp swelled in the pitch blackness. A moment of silence, then people started calling out to each other. Jemma felt along the counter for the walkie-talkie. 'The lights are out down here. Over.'

'Here too,' said Carl, his voice crackling. 'And the card reader. Over.'

What do I do? She blinked, and as her eyes adjusted to the darkness she saw the pale-green glow of the emergency light above the door to the stairs. 'OK, everyone who can reach their phone, please use the light or torch function and make your way to the door. Head for the green light. Please don't use the lift. We think it's a power cut.'

A thud, and someone swore. 'Please don't move until you can see where you're going,' she added. 'I don't believe this,' she muttered under her breath, but Luke didn't reply. She wasn't even sure he was there.

99

Gradually little beams of light switched on and she saw figures moving towards the exit. 'I'll go and open the door for them,' she said, and made her way over as best she could in the dim, flickering light.

Eventually, as far as she could tell, no one was left downstairs but herself and Luke, who stood motionless, holding his phone at arm's-length, the beam pointed down.

'I guess that's everyone,' she said. 'Come on, let's go upstairs. You first.'

Luke was silent, and she couldn't see his face; it was too dark. What on earth was going on? What had just happened? She had been so busy making sure that everyone was out of the room – and she really hoped they all were, because there was no way she could tell – that she hadn't had time to think about the situation.

'Luke,' she said, as they climbed the stairs, 'it's best that you go home. We won't be able to reopen until we get the power on.'

'Are you sure,' he said. It wasn't a question, more an agreement.

They emerged into the back room, which was almost as dark as downstairs, then into the main shop. Luke winced and put on his sunglasses. Jemma hadn't thought it was possible for him to be any paler, but his skin was greenish white. Carl was behind the counter, his face stricken. And standing in the middle of the room was Raphael. Jemma had never seen him look even mildly angry before, but now his face was twisted with rage.

'What has been going on?' He said it quietly, but Jemma squirmed, and her stomach churned.

'I think it's a power cut—' she said.

'I can see that,' he snapped. 'This whole section of the street is out.' Then his face changed. 'What else has happened?'

'We couldn't find books,' said Jemma. 'Not the ones that customers wanted.' She pointed to the box she had opened earlier, which was still sitting there, *Lost Horizon* on top.

Raphael glanced at the book, and his face looked as if it were carved from stone. 'Out, all of you!' he cried. 'Out, now!'

He marched into the back room, and the stockroom door smacked against the wall. Then he stormed back in. 'Didn't you hear me? I said get out!'

'I'm sorry,' murmured Luke. Without waiting for an answer, he opened the door and left. Jemma saw him jam his beanie hat on his head as he went past the window.

'Come on,' said Carl. He held the door for Jemma. 'Usual time tomorrow?' he asked Raphael.

Raphael stared at him blankly. 'Just *go*.' And as soon as they had stepped outside, he slammed the door and locked it. The sign turned from *Open* to *Closed*, and as Jemma watched, he pulled the blind down.

'Jemma.'

Jemma was still staring at the door of the bookshop. She jumped as Carl touched her arm.

'We need to go,' he said. '*You* need to go.'

She nodded, but didn't move.

He leaned closer. 'Can I get hold of someone for you?' he murmured.

Jemma looked at him. 'There isn't anyone, really,' she said. 'My family live a long way away, and—' For the first time in weeks, Em came into her mind. Em, who if they were still friends would have told her that she should have listened, and that Em had known this would happen, then probably taken her out to get drunk.

'Shall I take you home? Your home, I mean.'

Jemma thought of her flat, with its lumpy sofa-bed and depressing decor. Somehow, that didn't matter any more.

'Yes, please. If you don't mind—'

'Don't be silly,' said Carl. 'You'll have to tell me where we're going, though, because I've got no idea.'

'Embankment tube station,' said Jemma.

They walked without speaking; not fast, not slow. Occasionally Jemma looked at Carl. Sometimes he looked back, as if he felt her looking. 'We can talk later, if you want,' he said, once. 'There's no rush.'

They didn't really talk on the tube, either, except for Jemma to tell him her stop. And when they got outside and began walking again, everything felt unusual. The light was different, the smells were different. Shops normally open were closed, and the other way round. Jemma checked her watch; it was early afternoon. She told herself that was why things were strange. Carl strolled beside her, his long legs eating up the ground.

They turned into her road, and Jemma fumbled for her keys. 'Here we are,' she said, waving her hand at the once-grand townhouse. 'I'm on the top floor. Sorry.'

'Doesn't matter,' said Carl. 'It's a place of your own.'

'Yes,' said Jemma, and turned the key.

The *B* on her door was still wonky, which Jemma found somehow comforting. She let them in, glad that she had had a quick tidy round that morning, folded the sofa-bed up properly, and done the breakfast dishes. 'Would you like tea, or coffee?'

'Tea, please,' said Carl. 'Three sugars.'

Jemma's eyebrows shot up. 'Three?'

He grinned. 'I need the energy. Especially after today, and you should probably have an extra one, too. Isn't it supposed to be good for shock?'

'I'm not in—' said Jemma. Then she got two mugs out of the cupboard, and put the kettle on. A moment later she reopened the cupboard, reached to the back, and pulled out the untouched packet of emergency Bourbons. She checked the best-before date, grimaced, and put a few on a plate. If this wasn't the time for emergency biscuits, she didn't know when it would be.

'Thanks,' said Carl, when she handed him his mug. 'So…'

Jemma sat down in the opposite corner of the sofa. 'So, what?'

He met her eyes. 'Do you understand what happened today?'

Jemma shook her head, took a biscuit, eased the top off and dunked it in her tea. 'Not really. I mean, I've seen some things, of course I have, but – not like that.'

Carl put his mug down on the coffee table. 'What sort of things have you seen?'

So Jemma told him about the stock's mysterious habit of being exactly what was required, and the occasional changes of temperature and atmosphere, and the casual tricks the shop played on her when it was in the mood. The more she said, the deeper Carl's frown became.

'So you're saying that you think it's magic,' he said. 'The shop . . . is magic.'

Jemma shrugged. 'You have to admit it's the simplest explanation.' She sipped her sweet tea, screwed her mouth up, and reached for another biscuit. Then she caught sight of Carl's expression, and her hand stopped in mid-air.

'What?'

'But it can't be,' said Carl. He drank more tea, then put his mug down on the table with a clack. 'It just can't.'

'Yeah, I used to ignore it, too,' said Jemma. 'I used to tell myself that it was impossible, and that it must be a coincidence.' And then she told him about the underground river and the octopus.

Carl's frown now looked as if it would be permanently etched on his face. 'He came up soaking wet?'

'Yup,' said Jemma. 'He left a puddle on the floor. And when Raphael pulled the carpet back again, it had all disappeared.'

Carl huffed out a breath, shaking his head. 'OK. Fine.' He drank more tea. 'So we'll go along with the bookshop being magic, and possibly the cat, and maybe Raphael as well.' He grimaced as if he couldn't believe what he was saying. 'Even assuming all that, what happened today?'

'The shop reacted to Luke,' said Jemma. 'He looked terrible when he arrived, and he was really late. Either he was doing something the shop didn't like before he came to work, or else the shop tried to stop him getting there at all. When he did come in, it started misbehaving.'

'Yes, and it got worse when he pulled his phone out,' said Carl.

Jemma thought. 'Did he phone anyone, or did you see him send a message?'

'If he did, I didn't see him,' said Carl. 'He pulled the phone out, stared at it, then put it back in his pocket. I assume he got a message.'

'Well, short of confiscating his phone, we can't find out

what the message was,' said Jemma. 'I doubt he'll tell us.'

'That's if we ever see him again,' said Carl. 'He said sorry when he left, didn't he?'

Jemma stared at Carl. 'Do you think he'd just leave?'

It was Carl's turn to shrug. 'It's possible. And it was obviously him causing the trouble. But what did he do?'

Jemma thought of the missing books, and the box she had pulled out full of books with *Lost* in the title. 'Something's been lost,' she said, 'or taken. The minute Raphael saw what was in that box, he threw us out and went to the stockroom.'

'Which is full of books,' said Carl. 'Are any of them valuable?'

'Some will be,' said Jemma. 'Sometimes antiquarian booksellers visit him to buy books.' She told Carl about the deal he had struck with Brian, and the money that had changed hands. 'But while it's a lot of money for a book, it isn't megabucks. I mean, if you were picking any type of shop to steal from, you'd never choose a bookshop.'

'Not unless you really like books,' said Carl. 'Maybe that's why Raphael was so angry. It isn't that the books are particularly valuable, it's more that someone might have taken one.'

Jemma ran her finger around the rim of her cup. 'Luke likes the stockroom,' she said. 'He eats his lunch in there, and he scans books in there. He doesn't seem to like working upstairs in the shop, but he likes the stockroom.' She sighed. 'Maybe he has taken some books.'

'Could there be anything else in that room?' asked Carl. 'Maybe something you don't know about.'

Jemma managed a smile. 'If I don't know about it, then I wouldn't know.'

Carl grinned sheepishly. 'True. So what we've got is that Raphael is mad at us all, and probably going through everything in the stockroom right now to see what's left. Luke, I assume, won't show his face again, and he'll be sacked if he does.' He gazed into the middle distance, then shifted himself round to look at Jemma. 'Do you think the shop will carry on?'

Jemma stared at him, round-eyed. 'He can't close the shop! It's been there for ever! Raphael's run it for years. He won't close it over a book or two going missing.'

'Sorry,' said Carl. 'It was just – he looked so angry. I mean, no one would be pleased to come back to a power cut, then work out that someone's been helping themselves to stock, but he looked…' He frowned as he searched for the right word. 'Apocalyptic.'

Jemma shivered. She had put her pretty dress on that morning, and going by the weather forecast, hadn't bothered to add a cardigan or jacket. 'Excuse me a moment,' she said. She went to the corner cupboard, took out the first cardigan she saw, a thick cream one, and huddled herself in it. 'He can't close the shop,' she murmured. 'What would I do?'

Carl reached over and patted her woolly arm. 'Don't listen to me, I'm probably talking rubbish. And if he did, it wouldn't matter. You could get a job anywhere. You could manage another bookshop, or even open one of your own —'

'With what, exactly?' Jemma shot back. 'Look at this

place.' She waved her hand at the tired walls and drooping curtains. 'If I could afford to set up a bookshop in the middle of London, do you think I'd be living somewhere like this?'

'OK, it was just an idea,' said Carl. 'You could work in another bookshop. Whatever you wanted.'

Jemma stared at him, the lump in her throat growing bigger. 'I was let go,' she muttered.

Carl leaned closer. 'I'm sorry, I didn't catch that.'

'I was let go,' she enunciated very precisely. 'From my previous job. I was an analyst, and they made me redundant. Just me. Nobody else. I came in early, I went home late, and they still got rid of me. Finding the bookshop was a complete accident. And now I've messed that up too.' She hid her face in her hands and tried to stop her shoulders shaking.

She felt Carl shift closer, and with a careful hand he gave her shoulder a tentative rub. That made the floodgates open completely. She found a crumpled tissue in her pocket and did the best she could with it, though wiping her eyes seemed to make them stream even more. Carl continued to rub her shoulder gently, saying nothing.

Eventually Jemma cried herself out, managed to dab at her eyes once more with her soggy tissue, and apart from an occasional sniffle, was silent. 'Raphael doesn't know about that,' she whispered. 'That I was made redundant, I mean. I've never told him.'

'He doesn't need to know,' said Carl. 'And I don't think he'd care if he did. He's not that kind of guy.'

Jemma sighed a long, shuddery sigh. 'But what kind of

guy is he? I thought I knew him – well, as much as anyone does – but after today…'

'A couple of things are clear,' said Carl. 'Firstly, there's stuff in that stockroom you don't know about, and Raphael's worried that it's been taken. Secondly, the shop reckons that Luke's been up to no good – maybe stealing stuff, maybe something else – and it wants to get rid of him. And thirdly, Raphael is hopping mad and there's no point trying to talk to him until he's calmed down, which hopefully will be tomorrow.'

Jemma sat for a while, thinking. 'You forgot fourthly,' she said.

Carl raised an eyebrow. 'OK, what's fourthly?'

'Fourthly,' said Jemma, draining her mug and putting it down, 'we haven't had lunch and it's mid-afternoon. I don't know about you, but I'm hungry, and I want to forget all this for as long as I can.' A small smile tugged at the corners of her mouth, and finally succeeded in raising them a centimetre or so. 'So I think we should go out, get food, and watch a big stupid movie.'

Carl raised the other eyebrow. 'So let me get this straight. You're kind of inviting me for lunch and a movie?'

Jemma studied Carl's face. He didn't look horrified at the idea; in fact, he looked rather pleased. 'Yes, I am.'

He grinned. 'Just making sure. And yes, you're right; we definitely should. I can't think why I didn't include that in my summing up. But no scary movies, OK?'

Jemma laughed. 'OK.' And as she got up to wash her face and try and make herself look as if she hadn't been sobbing her heart out a few minutes earlier, she reflected that while the day had been, by anyone's standards, a complete disaster, that was only so far.

Chapter 15

Jemma rode the tube into central London the next morning with a sense of foreboding gnawing at her insides. Would Raphael let her in? Would the shop still be there? And what if Luke showed up?

She had arranged to meet Carl at Embankment tube station, and walk to the shop together. 'I know you could go alone,' Carl had said. 'I could, too. But it's – safer if we go together.'

Lunch had been pizza, at a place where Jemma had a discount card, followed by an early movie at a small cinema. During lunch they had avoided the subject of the shop entirely. Instead Carl had talked a little about his ambitions, the handful of acting jobs he had done, and Rumpus, the small theatre group he and a few ex-student friends had set up. 'But it's not just money that's the problem,' he said. 'Rehearsal space. Time to rehearse, even. We've all got jobs of sorts, and sometimes there's no room for anything else.'

'Maybe you could rehearse downstairs at the bookshop,' Jemma said, without thinking.

'Mmm,' said Carl. 'Anyway, that's enough about me. What do you do, besides work?'

Jemma briefly considered inventing an impressive hobby, like tapestry or wild swimming. Then she looked at Carl's face. *He's genuinely interested in me.*

'Not that much, really, apart from reading,' she said, nudging a pizza crust around her plate. 'My previous job took up a lot of time, and, well, you know what it's like.' She smiled. 'I'm getting into cooking, though.' She told him about the books she had borrowed, and the recipes she'd tried, and a couple of the disasters she'd had.

I probably shouldn't mention this, she thought, even as she was describing the world's driest Victoria sponge. But Carl laughed, and didn't seem bothered at all. 'That's one reason why I still live at home,' he said. 'Apart from not being able to afford my own place, my mum's cooking is awesome. Unlike mine.'

Carl saw her to the tube when the movie was over. 'Did you enjoy it?' he asked, when they were nearing the ticket barrier.

'They could have made more of the ending,' said Jemma. 'I was expecting a bigger explosion, to be honest.'

Carl smiled. 'I meant . . . this afternoon.'

Jemma felt herself flush pink, a sudden burn that shocked her. 'Of course I did! It was – it was just what I needed. Time away from – you know.'

'I know,' said Carl. 'Well, I suppose we should, um…'
He bit his lip. 'I'm not very good at this bit.'

'Neither am I,' said Jemma. 'I'll see you tomorrow,
about eight thirty. Um, yeah.' And, not quite sure if it was
what she ought to be doing, she stepped towards him,
stood on tiptoe, and kissed him on the cheek. Then she
moved away and busied herself getting her Oyster card out.
She hurried to the ticket barrier, head down, and only
looked back when she reached the stairs. Carl was
watching her, a little smile on his face. Jemma smiled,
waved, and disappeared.

***

Carl was waiting outside the tube station, as arranged.
'How are you feeling?' he asked.

'Nervous,' said Jemma. 'You?'

'Same.' He fell into step beside her. 'Mostly, I'm
hoping I still have a job.'

We ought to talk tactics, thought Jemma. *I ought to
have a plan.* She frowned. *Why don't I have a plan? I
always have a plan.*

You don't have a plan, said her annoying wiser self,
*because when you got home last night you ate toast,
watched crap on the telly, and flicked through Hello
magazine. How could you plan for this, anyway?*

Thanks for nothing. She pushed her inner voice back
into the cupboard and closed the door on her.

When they arrived at the bookshop, the blind was down
but the lights were on. Jemma and Carl exchanged glances.
'Guess we'd better knock,' said Jemma. She lifted the
knocker a little way, and executed three polite taps.

They waited. Jemma was about to knock again when she heard a key rattle in the lock. A few moments later, the door opened an inch or so and a blue eye blinked at them. 'Um, hello,' said Raphael.

'Hello,' said Jemma.

The door opened a little wider. 'Is it just you two?' asked Raphael.

'Yes,' said Carl.

The door swung open. They stepped in, and he locked the door behind them.

Jemma held her breath as she looked from Raphael to the shop. She had expected carnage; but to her surprise, everything seemed more or less in order. The shelves weren't quite as neat as usual, with some books sticking out a centimetre or two, and the counter could do with a polish, but otherwise… 'Have you had to do a lot of work?'

'I must apologise for yesterday,' said Raphael. 'I was worried about the stock, and I over-reacted. As it turns out, everything is as it should be, but I needed to send you home so that I could make absolutely sure.'

'But there are thousands of books in the stockroom,' said Jemma. 'It must have taken you all night.'

Raphael smiled thinly. 'Not if you know how to look,' he said. 'And luckily, I do. Shall I put the kettle on?'

'Not yet,' said Jemma. 'I'm glad nothing is missing, but what happened? Did you think something had been taken? What have you got in there, Raphael? *Is* it just books?'

She heard a small meow at her feet, glanced down, and gasped. 'What's happened to Folio?'

She crouched down and inspected the cat as she stroked him. Folio seemed a little smaller than usual, his fur rougher, and his usually pristine white paws were dusty. Even his eyes had lost a little of their shine. She tickled him under the chin and looked up at Raphael. 'What's going on?'

Raphael sighed. 'I had a feeling it would come to this.' He went into the back room. They heard running water, and the clack of mugs on the worktop. Raphael reappeared so suddenly that Jemma jumped. 'But you are both sworn to secrecy. Understand?'

'Yes,' they said, together.

Raphael's eyes moved to Carl. 'And the only reason that I'm telling you is because I suspect that if I don't, Jemma will tell you anyway.'

Raphael led them downstairs, and they sat at one of the café tables. 'I should have thought of this earlier,' said Raphael. 'Carl could have made us fancy drinks.'

'Please, Raphael,' said Jemma, shifting uncomfortably in her seat. 'Whatever it is, just tell us.'

Raphael fiddled with his spoon. 'It's not that easy,' he said. 'It isn't the sort of thing you tell people every day.'

Jemma looked at his hangdog expression. 'Is it really bad?' she asked. 'Will you get in trouble?'

Raphael stared at her. 'What do you mean? Of course I won't get in trouble. I'm one of the people *stopping* the trouble.'

Jemma stared back. 'What trouble?'

'Please tell us, Raphael,' said Carl. 'After yesterday, we're worried.'

115

'I understand that,' said Raphael. 'And I appreciate that you did your best. I daresay it would have been a lot worse if you two hadn't been in the shop.' He sat up straight and took a deep breath. 'The shop... The shop is not just a bookshop, but a repository of knowledge.'

Carl frowned. 'Well, yeah.'

Raphael smiled. 'I don't mean that in the usual sense. What I mean is that, as well as being a fairly normal secondhand bookshop, the shop also holds several more interesting volumes. These are sources and reference works for rare and arcane knowledge not available to the general public. Taken as single books, they are extremely valuable. But in certain combinations...' His gaze moved from Jemma to Carl, and back again. 'They are more powerful than you could imagine.'

Jemma picked up her mug and sipped automatically as she tried to comprehend what Raphael was saying. 'Is it secrets?' She considered her next word. 'Spells?'

'It can be anything, and everything,' said Raphael. 'Embargoed knowledge, banned books. Even marginalia; scribbled notes by the finest minds of the centuries.' He looked at their blank faces. 'OK, think of an egg.'

'*What?*' said Carl.

'No, go on, this will help,' said Raphael. 'Think of an egg. It's one thing, but you can combine it with other things in lots of different ways. So you could make an omelette, or a cake. Two very different things, but they both need the egg. So the books, and the pamphlets, and the other things which I keep are like special ingredients. You can combine them in all sorts of ways, and potentially,

116

do all sorts of things. And if my ingredients got into the wrong hands—'

'They could cook up something dangerous,' said Carl. 'OK, but why are the books kept here? Why not in the British Library?'

'That's where people would expect them to be,' said Raphael. 'So obviously you'd never put them there. Let's face it, who'd think this place had anything except for lightly used mass-market books?'

'So the shop is a front,' said Jemma. She drank some more tea. Her head was beginning to swim. 'And when you said you didn't want people coming here and asking questions, and you wanted the shop to stay in balance, that was why.'

'That's exactly it,' said Raphael.

'Oh,' said Jemma. A wave of guilt swept over her, and she blinked. 'So, this thing with Luke yesterday… Do you think he tried to steal something?'

Raphael sighed. 'I don't know. On balance, I think not. The shop thinks he's up to no good, clearly.' He rubbed his nose. 'I wanted to give him a chance, even though I could see there might be problems. But it's backfired.'

'Do you think,' said Jemma, in a small voice, 'that it's happened because – because of things I did? Because the shop's doing better now?'

'No,' said Raphael. 'Well, not directly. The changes to the shop may have accelerated the process, but I'm sure it would have happened anyway. These things do occur every so often, and there's not much I can do about it except stay alert.'

Jemma felt as if a huge weight had been lifted off her. 'So what do you *do*, exactly?'

Raphael considered, stirring his tea absently as he did so. 'Without going into unnecessary detail, I'm a Keeper. I store the knowledge sources I possess in optimum conditions, far enough apart so that no adverse reactions can occur, and occasionally I acquire new ones.'

'But the stockroom isn't even locked,' said Jemma.

'It doesn't need to be,' said Raphael. 'If an unauthorised person tried to take a knowledge source, things would happen.'

'Is that what happened yesterday?' asked Jemma. 'With all the lost and gone and missing books?'

'Not quite, no,' said Raphael. 'But I was worried that someone with strong skills might have bypassed the security somehow. What you saw yesterday was not an alert, but a warning. Throwing you out was a precaution, really.'

'When you say strong skills,' said Carl, 'I take it you don't mean that they're handy with a crowbar, or at picking a lock.'

Raphael smiled. 'No, no. In our line of work, things are different.'

'So there's more than one of you?' asked Jemma.

'Oh yes,' said Raphael. 'It would be a terribly hard job to keep hold of all the powerful writings in the world, wouldn't it? Apart from anything else, you'd need an awful lot of room to store them properly, without repercussions. No, there are people like me in cities all over the world. New York, and Paris, and Athens, and so on.'

'So you're the Keeper for London,' said Jemma. She felt as if she were standing on the point of a pin, on top of the Empire State Building, in a high wind. The world that she thought she knew had changed utterly.

'Sort of,' said Raphael. 'There was talk of moving HQ to somewhere else, like Birmingham or Oxford or Manchester, but everyone agreed that with so many bookshops in London it would be foolish to shift it. So I'm based in London, but I look after England, in general. Not just me, I have Assistant Keepers too. Some here, some in other places.'

'Wow,' said Carl, gazing at Raphael as if he'd never seen him before. 'So you're, like, the Keeper for England?'

Raphael made a rueful face. 'It is a bit ridiculous, isn't it? But yes, that's me.' He drank half his mug of tea in one go. 'That wasn't as bad as I thought it would—'

They jumped at a knock on the door upstairs. 'That's weird,' said Carl. 'I mean, I can't usually hear the door down here.'

'Yes,' said Raphael. Suddenly, his face was stern. 'And the fact that we can still hear it loud and clear means that I know exactly who it is.'

Chapter 16

'What do we do?' asked Jemma. 'It's Luke, isn't it?'

'We go upstairs,' said Raphael, 'and we let him in. And then we ask him what exactly he's been doing.'

Jemma realised as she climbed the steps that she was still clutching her mug as if it would protect her. She put it in the sink as they went through the back room, and wiped her hands on her jeans. She felt shivery at the thought of the confrontation that was about to take place.

Raphael, however, seemed calm; jaunty, even. 'Perhaps he will be able to explain himself,' he said. 'I doubt it, though.' He unlocked the door and flung it open.

Luke stood on the doorstep. His shoulders drooped, his head was bowed, and his hair hung in lank tendrils. He looked as if he had been crying. 'I wasn't sure you'd open the door to me,' he muttered.

Raphael eyed him. 'You don't seem particularly

dangerous,' he said. 'Are you coming in, or what?'

'You're letting him come in?' said Jemma. 'After yesterday?'

'Yes, I am,' said Raphael. 'Luke ought to be given a chance to explain, and I for one would like to know more about the possible reasons for yesterday's events.' He motioned towards the interior of the shop, and Luke walked meekly in.

'I'm watching you,' said Jemma. 'Raphael may be prepared to talk to you, but I'm not sure I am.'

Raphael looked at her, an eyebrow raised. 'Jemma, if you could leave this to me.' He turned to Luke. 'What did you do yesterday?' He indicated the armchair. 'Sit down, please, and tell me.'

Luke eyed the chair, and blinked. 'Can we go downstairs?'

Raphael glanced at the window. 'I don't think that's necessary. Sit down, Luke, and explain.'

Luke shrugged. 'I didn't do anything,' he said, and flopped into the armchair. 'I don't know why it all happened.'

'You must have done something,' said Jemma. 'The shop was perfectly normal until you came in, what was it, three hours late?'

'I—' Luke swallowed. 'I got held up.'

Jemma snorted, but at another glance from Raphael she said no more.

'Jemma's right,' said Carl. 'You showed up, and everything turned weird. Even the air was weird. And books went missing, and the customers were fighting, and

121

then there was a power cut.' He gave Luke a hard stare. 'You did something, man.'

Luke raised his hands, and let them fall on the arms of the chair. 'I didn't,' he said. 'I just tried to do my best with the customers, and everything kept going wrong.'

Raphael was staring at him too. 'Let's say, for a moment, that you didn't do anything you shouldn't have yesterday,' he said. 'Why would the shop make things difficult for you? Why might it want to stand in your way?' He caught Jemma's pleading look. 'Luke is an intelligent young man. I'm sure he is perfectly aware that this is not a normal shop, so I won't pretend that it is.' He waited. 'I'll give you one more chance, and that's it.'

Luke's hands tightened on the arms of the chair. 'I didn't do anything yesterday,' he said. 'Or the day before, or the day before that. The only time I did do anything was in the first week. I was on trial, and I figured it didn't matter, because you probably wouldn't keep me on.'

Jemma felt the blood drain from her face, and put a hand on the counter to steady herself. 'What did you do?' she asked, her mouth dry.

'I wish you wouldn't look at me like that,' said Luke, irritably. 'It wasn't anything terrible. It was just – I passed on some information, that was all. To another bookseller.'

Raphael took a step closer. 'Now we're getting somewhere,' he said. 'What sort of information?'

'He wanted to know how the shop was organised – or not organised.' He smiled, briefly. 'And he asked me to find out and tell him what sort of stock you had, and where you were buying books.'

Raphael held his gaze. 'Did you?'

'Not after the first week,' said Luke. 'You were all so nice to me, and I felt as if – as if I belonged. Which I've probably wrecked now.' His pale-green eyes rested on them in turn. 'The bookseller kept badgering me for more information, and after a while I fed him fake stuff. I don't think he guessed.'

Carl frowned. 'When you were looking at your phone yesterday, was it a message from him?'

Luke nodded. 'It was.'

'And who is this mysterious bookseller?' asked Raphael.

Luke took a long time to answer. 'I can't tell you. I'm sorry, but I can't.'

'We could get his phone, maybe, and find out that way,' said Carl, moving forward a little.

Raphael shook his head. 'No, we won't be doing that.'

'All right, let's call the police, then,' said Jemma, eyeing the Bakelite phone nearby.

'Again, that's a no,' said Raphael. 'We can deal with this perfectly well on our own.' He studied Luke. 'I assume this – person has a hold over you, and that's why you won't give me his name.' He checked his watch. 'Well, it's five past nine, and given that we lost most of yesterday afternoon's trading, we should open up.' He walked to the window and threw up the blind. 'I'll run things here. Jemma, please go downstairs with Carl.'

'That's it?' Jemma stared at Luke, who first looked away, then hid his face in his hands. 'You're going to let him stay?'

Raphael glanced at him before replying. 'The shop doesn't seem bothered by him today, so provided he stays somewhere we can keep an eye on him, it shouldn't be a problem.' He smiled. 'And if he's been feeding false information to an enemy, it may even be useful to keep him.'

Jemma was still shaking her head in disbelief as he turned the sign on the front door. 'I give up,' she murmured. Carl reached for her hand, and squeezed it.

They looked up as the door opened. 'Oh, I'm so glad you're open,' said a reedy voice. An elderly lady shuffled in, her stick thunking on the parquet. 'I was here yesterday, but unfortunately you had a power cut and I wasn't able to buy the book I wanted.'

'Yes, sorry about that,' said Jemma. 'Which book was it?'

'*Excellent Women*, by Barbara Pym.' She said the name very precisely. 'I think I put it on one of the little tables.'

'I'll go and see,' said Jemma. 'I shouldn't be long.'

She ran downstairs, and tensed for a moment as she opened the great oak door; but behind it, things appeared normal. The lights were on, and the lower floor was its usual imposing but welcoming self. Jemma took a deep, experimental breath. Yes, the air was fresher. She sighed with relief. Raphael had cleared the tables and re-shelved the books, but *Excellent Women* was shelved under P in General Fiction, just as it should be.

She took the book upstairs and handed it to Raphael. 'Would you mind serving this lady, please? I'll take a couple of boxes down, then we're all set.'

'Good idea,' said Raphael. He looked inside the cover. 'That will be two pounds, please. Would you like a bag?'

Jemma went to the stockroom and chose a box on which Luke had written *CRIME* in neat capitals. *Will it have crime books in it, though? Might he have mislabelled it to confuse us?* She couldn't work out what was most likely. *The easiest way is to open it and see.*

She took the box through to the shop, and hunted for the scissors. Luke turned his head, and at the sight of the box he relaxed.

Jemma snipped at the tape holding the box closed and peeled it off, then lifted the flaps and peered inside. Her brow furrowed. 'That isn't what I expected.'

Raphael leaned over and looked into the box. He glanced at Jemma, then pushed the flaps closed. 'Is that everything for today?' he asked the customer.

She giggled. 'Oh yes, just the one today, but I'm sure you'll see me again.' She beamed at them all, then began to thunk towards the door. Raphael came out from behind the counter, scurried around her, and held the door open. As soon as she had gone, he locked it.

'Mind if I open it now?' asked Jemma, with rather a resentful look. She reached in, took out the first book, and laid it on the counter.

Dracula.

'What the—' cried Luke. 'I put crime books in there, I know I did!'

She reached in again.

Interview with a Vampire.

Twilight.

A *Buffy the Vampire Slayer* novelisation.

'I don't believe it,' Luke whispered, his face pale as death. 'This bloody shop.'

Carl looked at the books, then at Luke, then back at the books. He blinked, several times. Then he stared at Luke. 'You're a vampire?'

Luke gazed at him miserably, and said nothing.

'That's why you don't like working upstairs, isn't it?' said Jemma. 'Because of the light. And that's why you dived under the counter when Stella took a photo of you. And why you don't ever eat lunch with us.' She shook her head. 'I – I don't know what to say.'

Luke's eyes moved from one to the other of them. His bottom lip started to tremble, and he burst into sobs. Apart from his noisy crying, the room was completely silent.

Chapter 17

Jemma looked at Carl, who shrugged, his expression nonplussed. Then she eyed Raphael, who was watching Luke. He didn't appear remotely surprised. 'How did you know?' she asked.

'I wasn't sure at first,' said Raphael. 'I had a suspicion at the interview, and subsequent events bore it out.'

Luke's sobs were beginning to ease a little, and the space between them was growing. Raphael took a large white handkerchief from his trouser pocket and touched Luke's hand with it. Luke grabbed it, buried his face in it, and continued to cry more quietly.

Jemma wasn't sure what to think. *Should I be scared?* But Luke wasn't scary in the slightest. As for biting people – if anything, he seemed to prefer being alone. She thought over his interactions with her, and concluded that maybe she just wasn't his blood type. Or type, full stop.

While that was a relief, she had to admit to feeling the tiniest bit offended.

'Erm, would anyone like a cup of tea?' she asked. 'I know we've just had one, but—'

'What a good idea,' said Raphael. 'Why don't you and Carl go and make it?' When he spoke again, his voice was softer. 'Luke, would you like a cup of tea?'

Luke's shoulders stiffened, then he said, through the handkerchief, 'Yes please. Could I have decaf?'

'We'll go and do that, then,' said Jemma. 'Come on, Carl.' He was still gazing at Luke, with an expression that suggested he didn't know what to do with him. She touched his arm, and pointed towards the back room.

'This place is doing my head in,' whispered Carl, as Jemma filled the kettle. 'First magic, now vampires.'

Jemma looked at him. 'Are you scared? I feel as if I should be, but I'm not.'

'I haven't had time to be scared,' said Carl. 'I mean, I thought vampires were meant to be all dramatic and creepy and dangerous, but he's just pale and weedy.' He leaned closer. 'You don't think Raphael is a vampire, do you? I mean, they say it takes one to know one.'

'I doubt it,' said Jemma. 'If he craves anything, it's pastry and caffeine. And then there's his clothes. At least Luke dresses in black.' She smiled. 'Thinking about it now, I can't believe I didn't spot it. But then, everyone knows that vampires aren't real.' She snorted. 'Then again, I didn't believe in magic six months ago.'

'I wonder what Raphael's saying to him,' said Carl.

'Your guess is as good as mine,' said Jemma. She

hoped that, whatever it was, Luke would have stopped crying when they went back in. It was awful watching other people cry, particularly when you had a suspicion that you might be partly responsible.

Jemma let the tea brew for quite a while before taking the tray through. When she did, she found Raphael crouching beside Luke's chair, speaking quietly. He saw her, murmured something, then stood up and moved back a little. While Luke looked forlorn and wan, and still let out an occasional hiccup, he appeared much calmer. He accepted the mug that Jemma handed to him, and sipped slowly.

'Luke and I have had a chat,' said Raphael. Jemma and Carl exchanged glances. 'He has assured me that he is a non-practising vampire.'

Jemma frowned. 'Can you do that? I mean, don't you die?'

Luke shot her a pained glance.

'OK, I'm sorry if that's a stupid question,' she said. 'I'm not particularly knowledgeable about vampires. Until now, I haven't needed to be.'

'You're quite safe,' said Luke, with a thin smile. 'I've been clean for over three hundred years. That's the last time I bit a human.'

Carl stared. 'But you look like you're about my age.'

Luke's smile broadened a little. 'That's one of the few benefits, I suppose.'

'So how do you manage without biting people?' asked Jemma.

Luke's eyes narrowed. Then he shrugged. 'You've

probably noticed I carry a drinks bottle with me.'

Jemma gasped. 'Don't tell me it's—'

'No it is *not*,' said Luke. 'I drink a blood substitute. It has the same nutrients as blood, and looks and tastes fairly similar, but actually it's vegan.'

'Vegan blood?' said Carl. 'Where do you get that, the health-food shop?'

Luke smiled. 'You can get anything off the internet. I also eat raw meat when it's convenient, which it often isn't. And when I'm absolutely desperate, I go and find a pigeon. Trafalgar Square's handy for that. They're nice and plump because the tourists feed them.'

'So there are probably vampire pigeons in Trafalgar Square?' Jemma grabbed her own mug of tea and drank deep.

Carl grinned. 'Yeah, but have you ever been pecked by a pigeon?'

'Exactly,' said Luke. 'I figured they were less dangerous than rats.'

'But—' Jemma felt as if her brain was overheating. 'But what happens if the pigeon eats a worm? Or half a worm? Would the bit that didn't get eaten be a vampire worm? Then what?'

Raphael laughed. 'Jemma, you may be overthinking things.'

'Maybe,' snapped Jemma. 'But you can't expect me to say fine, my colleague is a vampire, and accept it. I mean, until today I didn't believe vampires were real, and now I'm drinking tea with one.' She looked at Luke, whose head had drooped again, and immediately felt guilty.

'Luke, I'm sorry if I'm not taking this very well. It's just – vampires get a bad press, you know? I've never met one before. To be honest, you're not what I would have expected.'

He gazed up at her, doubt in his eyes.

'I don't mean that in a bad way,' she said hastily. 'I mean, you seem nice. And a good colleague, when the shop isn't messing about. So I suppose I have to get used to the idea that one of my colleagues happens to be a vampire. And if you don't bite people, then I guess that's OK.'

Luke smiled, then blinked, and a tear rolled down his cheek. 'It means a lot to hear you say that,' he said. 'I'd like to be honest with people, course I would, but when you've been hounded and threatened and had people running after you with stakes as much as I have, you learn to keep quiet.' Then his mouth wobbled again. 'I don't think the shop's prepared to accept me, though. I mean, it outed me.'

Raphael's brow furrowed as he thought. 'The thing with the shop,' he said, 'is that it doesn't really consider people's feelings, even though it's quite sensitive itself. In this case, I suspect the shop had seen what you were, and knew what you had been doing, and sensed that the two were linked. So it concluded that the best way to sort things out was to bring into the open the thing it *could* reveal – that you are a vampire – in the hope that the other matter would follow.' He licked a finger and held it up. 'See how calm the shop is now.'

'That doesn't make it right,' said Jemma. 'And in front

of a customer, too.'

Raphael seemed to be considering his answer. 'Maybe the shop trusts us to do the right thing,' he said. 'That said, what is the right thing to do?'

'Well, if the shop isn't being weird with Luke, and he isn't stealing stuff or leaking information, then he can stay,' said Jemma. 'If he wants to.' She looked at Luke. 'Do you want to?'

'Of course I want to,' said Luke. 'I love working here. Now you know, and you're OK with it, and—' He spread his hands wide and smiled. 'I'm really happy. No one has a hold over me any more, and you don't know how good that feels.'

'Oh yes!' cried Jemma. 'You can tell us who the bookseller is!'

'Yes, I can,' said Luke, and suddenly he was grave. 'And I'm afraid it's someone you know.'

'I thought as much,' said Raphael. 'How did he find you? And how did he know about you?'

'Family connection,' said Luke. 'He's my great-great-nephew. Obviously he's known me a long time, and known *of* me, and I guess when he needed someone to spy for him, I was the obvious choice. He made me an offer I couldn't refuse. "Do what I ask," he said, "or I'll expose you for what you are, and you'll have to start all over again somewhere else. If they let you live, that is."' The corner of his mouth twisted up. 'For years I've worked on resisting a lot of the usual dangers, like crucifixes and holy water. Sunlight, to a degree, though as you've seen it makes me uncomfortable. I can even eat a clove of garlic, which gives me mild indigestion. Unfortunately, instilling fear and suspicion and hatred in other people still works like a charm. He knows that only too well, and I doubt he hesitated for a second.'

Jemma's eyebrows shot up. 'And he's family? What sort of person would do that to you?'

Luke sipped some more tea. 'A man who is on a mission. He has one ambition, and he will stop at nothing to fulfil it. The Assistant Keeper for Westminster, or as I think of him, my great-great-nephew, Brian.'

Chapter 18

'I knew Brian was dodgy!' cried Jemma.

'You didn't say anything,' said Raphael, with a gleam in his eye.

'That's because I thought it was just me,' said Jemma. 'I mean, you can't go accusing people, but that time when he came in and you sold him that book, I could feel that you two didn't get on.' She turned to Luke. 'So what is he trying to do?'

'Take Raphael's job,' said Luke. 'He told me that from the start. He was completely open about it. That's the sort of person he is.'

'But how?' said Jemma. 'I mean, what will he do, walk in and say "I want your job?" Or is he going to, I don't know, accuse you of something and take you to a tribunal or – or what?'

'Your first answer was pretty much right,' said Raphael.

'Appointment to these positions is pretty informal, and one can be challenged at any time. And yes, Brian could walk in here in the next ten minutes, say, "I challenge you," and kick things off. I don't think he will – not yet – but I've sensed something in the air for a little while.'

'But what *happens*?' said Jemma. She felt as if her grip on reality might be slipping. 'I mean, do you play conkers, or joust, or cast spells—'

'What we do,' said Raphael, 'is we put on our ceremonial robes, and stand on adjacent mountain tops, and throw spells at each other.'

Jemma's jaw dropped.

Raphael chuckled. 'I just wanted to see if you'd swallow that. I'm afraid it's much more prosaic. Basically, it's a duel of knowledge. We are each allowed to present three books. The challenger goes first, and we present the books one by one in turn, announcing the name and author. Once the opponent has verified that the book is what its owner says it is, the book is accepted. The strongest set of three books is victorious. That doesn't necessarily mean the strongest three books will win, though. If you remember what I was saying the other day, it's all about the combination; the three books have to work well together. So using our cake analogy, eggs, butter and flour will work better together than eggs, sardines and jam.'

Jemma made a face. 'OK, I get that. So once the winner is decided, what happens then?'

'It's pretty straightforward,' said Raphael. 'If the incumbent, in this case me, wins, then their post is retained. If Brian wins, he takes my job and everything that goes with it. Except Folio. Folio is a personal item.'

Jemma gasped. 'So he'd get the shop?'

'Yes, he would. And depending on what sort of mood he was in, he could choose to keep you on in his employment, or let you go.'

'I'd never work for Brian,' said Jemma. She nudged Carl.

'No, neither would I,' he said, quickly.

'And I definitely wouldn't,' said Luke. 'I managed a week of doing his bidding, and that was only because he forced me into it.'

'That's very touching,' said Raphael. 'I am sorry to put you in this position.'

'If he takes your shop,' said Jemma, 'what happens to you?'

'The rules are clear,' said Raphael. 'The loser is banished from their former sphere of influence for ten years. So in my case, that would be England.'

'That's horrible,' said Carl.

'Them's the rules,' said Raphael. 'Anyway, I believe that Llandudno is very nice at this time of year. Perhaps I could open a little bookshop there while I regroup.'

'But this is your life!' cried Jemma. 'This bookshop's been in your family for ages, you said.' A sudden thought occurred to her, and her eyes narrowed as realisation dawned. 'Hang on a minute. If Brian is Luke's great-great-nephew – and I'm ignoring how weird that is – and Luke is at least three hundred years old, then Brian must be pretty old too. Agreed?'

'Agreed,' said Raphael. 'I perceive the cogs are turning.'

'And you said you were selling books before Brian,' said Jemma. 'So how old are you?'

Raphael smiled. 'I'm as old as my tongue, and a little older than my teeth. To be completely honest with you, I've lost count. After the first couple of hundred, birthdays do get a bit samey.'

'I imagine they would,' murmured Carl. 'I mean, there's only so many pairs of socks you can wear.'

'That's true,' said Raphael. 'I won't need any more socks for at least fifty years. Clothes are different, because fashions change, but socks tend to stay with you.'

'Never mind socks, what are we going to do?' said Jemma. 'You can't lose the bookshop, you just can't!'

'I could,' said Raphael. 'How do you think I got it in the first place?'

Jemma's mouth dropped open. 'You didn't,' she said.

'I'm afraid I did,' said Raphael. 'I challenged the previous Keeper of England in 1812. The Napoleonic Wars were going on, everyone was a bit distracted, and I'm afraid I took advantage of that. He was getting on a bit, though. Very set in his ways. Never liked printed books. He had some lovely illuminated manuscripts, but there's only so far you can go with most of those. Anyway.' He smiled at the three of them. 'I certainly don't intend to go without a fight. Brian is clearly working himself up for a challenge, and I intend to be a little more ready than he thinks.'

'You're absolutely right, Raphael,' said Luke. 'He told

me to give him information on any book that looked – what was the word – venerable.'

Raphael chuckled. 'Ever the antiquarian, Brian. It's one of the things I occasionally chide him for, and he always bristles.' Then his smile faded. 'What did you tell him?'

'I didn't see much in the first week that I could tell him about,' said Luke. 'And since I decided I wasn't playing his game any more, I've told him that most of your stock is cheap paperbacks with an occasional modern first edition.'

'Excellent,' said Raphael. He rubbed his hands. 'I'm sure that Brian was heartened by that news, but we can encourage him still further. Would you mind going to the stockroom and taking out – well, any box.'

Luke stared at him. 'Any box?'

'Yes,' said Raphael. 'I'm sure it will have just the thing.'

Luke looked at him for a long moment. 'If you say so,' he said. He pushed himself out of the armchair, and walked into the back room. Then he popped his head round the door. 'It will let me in, won't it? Nothing will . . . happen?'

'I doubt it,' said Raphael. 'I'd watch out for Folio, though, if he's around. I think he's a little upset with his condition. Hopefully that will improve soon.'

'So Folio and the shop are – sort of bound together?' asked Jemma.

'They are,' said Raphael. 'I rescued Folio from a sack in the Thames, and living in the bookshop is all he knows. I don't know what would happen if he left it.' His face darkened. 'But I wouldn't leave him here with Brian.'

Jemma bit her lip and stared hard at the opening to the back room. Carl's hand slipped into hers, and she curled her fingers round his. He drew her a little closer, and she rested her head against his shoulder. She felt a little better, but not much.

Luke reappeared with a box and put it on the counter. 'Shall I open it?' he asked.

'Usually I'd say yes,' said Raphael, 'but on this occasion, perhaps not.' He got the scissors, slit the box open, and brought out a large, black, leather-bound tome. He blew the dust off it, and regarded it critically. 'Yes, lovely. He *will* like this.' He showed them the spine.

'Lyell, *Principles of Geology*, Volume 1,' read Carl.

'That's the one,' said Raphael. 'First edition, published in 1830. But the important thing about this book is that it was read, and at the same time annotated, by Charles Darwin.'

'*The* Charles Darwin?' said Carl. 'Who used to be on the ten-pound note?'

'The very same,' said Raphael. 'Luke, I want you to take a picture of the title page. That will tell Brian what the book is, and…' He opened the book and they saw, at the top right of the page, a small, neat signature. 'That will seal the deal. I'd like you to send Brian the picture, with the message: *You'll never believe what he's got.*'

'Won't that give him an advantage?' said Jemma. 'He'll know you've got it.'

'He will,' said Raphael. 'What he doesn't know is that I have no intention of using it. I have a combination of books in my head, but this is not one of them.'

'So it's a red herring?' asked Carl.

'Precisely,' said Raphael, and smiled a contented smile. 'Jemma, I have a job for you, too.' He reached into the box and brought out another book. This one was slimmer, and bound in maroon cloth. 'Have you ever heard of a place called Sir John Soane's Museum?'

'No, sorry,' said Jemma. 'I'm not a big fan of museums.'

Raphael rolled his eyes. 'I despair of young folk sometimes, I really do,' he said. 'Anyway. Look it up on the internet. It isn't far away, in Holborn. What I want you to do is stroll round – it doesn't open till ten – ask to see the Assistant Curator, and give her this book, along with a note that I shall write for you. She will give you another book in exchange. Put it in your bag, then return as quickly as you can. If at all possible, take a taxi. It is absolutely imperative that you lose no time.'

Jemma swallowed. 'OK.'

'And what about me?' asked Carl. 'Do you have a job for me?'

'Oh yes,' said Raphael. 'We must reopen the shop shortly, as I wish everything to appear as normal as it ever is in this place, and we shall be a shop manager down. During Jemma's hopefully short absence, I shall run things up here. Luke, I shall need you downstairs. And Carl, I shall require you to supply me with strong coffee and items of sugary pastry at regular intervals. I have a lot of thinking to do, and I need to keep my strength up.'

Carl grinned. 'You're on. I don't know much about books, but hot beverages and pastry are absolutely my thing.' Then he looked worried. 'But we haven't got any fresh stuff in yet. Have I got time to go round to Rolando's before Jemma leaves?'

'Of course,' said Raphael. 'Oh, and could you ask Giulia if she could include some cinnamon rolls?'

Jemma frowned. 'Don't you mean Rolando?'

'Not on this occasion,' said Raphael. 'She knows that if I use her name, it's important. Believe me, her cinnamon rolls have powers that you can only dream of.'

Carl's eyes widened. 'You mean they're magical?'

'No.' Raphael grinned. 'But they are exceptionally tasty, and I always do my best thinking with a cinnamon roll in my hand. And today, to get the better of Brian, the very best thinking is required.'

Chapter 19

Jemma stared doubtfully at the Georgian townhouse before her. It didn't look like any museum she'd ever visited. It just looked like a nice big house in a leafy London square.

Carl had returned from Rolando's with two trays of pastries and Giulia herself, who was clutching a brown-paper bag and a book. She burst through the front door and immediately hurled a stream of Italian at Raphael, thrusting the bag and the book at him. He held his hands up, then, after a rapid exchange of Italian, he took her into the back room.

'I'd better go,' said Jemma. 'You two, get ready to open.'

And now she was at her destination. A young man in jeans and an open-necked white shirt stood at the entrance. 'Are you coming in?' he asked.

'Yes, please,' said Jemma. 'Do I need to pay?'

'No, it's free.' He smiled at her. 'But could you switch off your mobile phone' – he eyed the phone in her hand – 'and put your bag in the cloakroom.'

'Ah,' said Jemma. 'There could be a slight problem with that. I have a note and a book for the Assistant Curator.'

A tiny crease appeared between the young man's eyebrows. 'In that case, the best thing to do is to take the book and the note out, and someone in the shop will summon the AC.' He nodded, seemingly pleased with his solution, and handed her a clear plastic bag. Jemma did as she had been told, and proceeded inside.

The shop was to her left past the cloakroom, all art books and curios and pretty jewellery. Jemma explained to the shop assistant, who picked up the telephone. She spoke quietly into the receiver, then listened. 'I'm sorry,' she said to Jemma, 'but who did you say you were?'

'I didn't, but I'm Jemma James, from Burns Books.'

The shop assistant relayed this information, listened once more, then replaced the receiver gently in its cradle. 'She's on her way,' she said. 'If you'd like to go into the next room, she will meet you there.'

Jemma wandered into the next room, which was lined with books. *What a house to live in*, she thought. It was dark, probably to preserve the items within. She was studying a painting on an easel when a small cough made her jump. A few feet away stood a petite woman with a shiny black bob, wearing black trousers and a cream blouse with little blue flowers on. 'Jemma James?' she asked, holding out her hand. 'I am the Assistant Curator.

Please come this way.' She took Jemma first down into the kitchen, then into one of the strangest rooms that Jemma had ever seen. If she had thought the gift shop was full of items, it was nothing compared to this. Statues and busts and stone mouldings stood everywhere, and in the middle was a giant sarcophagus.

'He was quite a collector,' said the Assistant Curator.

'I can see that,' said Jemma. From this room they went up a different set of stairs, then into a room which seemed to be a library. To be honest, Jemma wasn't sure what anything was. 'Is this where the book is?' she asked.

The Assistant Curator didn't answer, but went to one of the bookshelves and pressed a knot in the wood. The bookshelf opened like a cupboard, and she beckoned Jemma through.

On the other side of the door was a small library of perhaps five hundred books. The rest of the room was painted white, and its lack of decoration, in contrast to the rooms Jemma had passed through, made it seem even more bare. In the corner stood a small desk and two chairs. The Assistant Curator waved Jemma to one, and took the other herself. 'May I see your note, please?'

Jemma handed it over. She had thought it odd that Raphael had addressed it to *Assistant Curator*, rather than by name, but now she wondered whether the Assistant Curator had a name at all. Or was she a sort of Keeper, too? The woman picked up a plain silver letter-opener, slit the envelope, and skimmed through the note rapidly. Her expression did not change.

'I see,' she said. 'I'm afraid there is a small problem.'

144

Jemma's heart plummeted not to her boots, but to the basement kitchen. 'What sort of problem?' she breathed.

'I do apologise,' said the Assistant Curator. 'If I had the book I would gladly give it to you, but it isn't here.'

'Has someone taken it?' Suddenly it was hard to breathe. 'Has an old man visited you? A tall, stooping man with a big white moustache?'

The Assistant Curator regarded her for a long moment. 'It's being restored,' she said. 'We take the best care of the books that we can, but they still deteriorate. It's with a specialist bookbinder in Edinburgh. Well, to be quite honest, it's probably somewhere in the postal system, as we only sent it yesterday.'

If it's in the postal system, thought Jemma, *I doubt even magic can bring it back.* She blinked. 'This is the book Raphael asked me to bring you,' she said, proffering it. 'I don't suppose you have anything similar to the book he asked for?'

The Assistant Curator took the book, inspected it, and re-read the letter. Then she put both on the desk, clasped her hands in front of her, and mused. 'Is everything all right at the bookshop?' she asked.

What should I tell her? What am I allowed to tell her? Jemma wished she had her phone with her, and could consult with Raphael. Then she remembered that Raphael had told her to be quick. 'We think something's going to happen at the bookshop,' she gabbled. 'That's why Raphael wants to swap the books.' She felt even more flustered under the calm gaze of the Assistant Curator.

'I see.' The pause lengthened to a minute. Then the

Assistant Curator rose, went to one of the bookshelves, and drew out a curiously shaped book bound in sky blue. It was slim, and much wider than it was tall. 'I'm not sure this will do exactly the same job as the book Raphael wanted,' she said, 'but it may be a good alternative.' She opened the drawer of the desk and drew out a canvas tote bag with the museum's logo on, then slipped the sky-blue book and Jemma's book inside. She pushed it across the desk to Jemma, and got up. 'I'll take you back down,' she said.

'Do I need to sign something?' asked Jemma. 'Or – or fill in a form?'

The Assistant Curator smiled a wintry smile. 'I won't forget. And good luck.'

Jemma hurried through the museum, lingered for a second as she saw some nice earrings in the shop, then reclaimed her bag, put the tote inside it, and stepped out into the not-still air.

A black cab was waiting outside. 'Jemma James?' the driver called.

Jemma nodded. 'Charing Cross Road, please.'

'Don't worry,' said the cabbie. 'I know exactly where you're meant to be.'

London was remarkably quiet, and the journey back to the shop took just a few minutes. Jemma tried to pay the cabbie, who waved her purse away. 'Prepaid, innit,' he said. As soon as she was out of the cab, he drove off.

She turned to the shop and saw Raphael in the doorway. 'Come in, Jemma, quickly. Did you get it?'

Jemma bit her lip, and shook her head. 'It's gone for

binding,' she said. 'But the Assistant Curator gave me another book instead, and let me keep yours.' She walked into the shop and found Luke and Carl standing there. She opened her bag and handed the tote to Raphael. He peeped within, then went to the shop door and locked it.

'Why are you both upstairs?' asked Jemma. 'What about the customers?'

'There aren't any,' said Carl. 'We had a couple, early doors, then nothing. It's as if the shop knows.'

'It's as well you came back when you did,' said Raphael. 'I have a feeling that if you'd been five or ten minutes later, you wouldn't have been able to get near.'

'What do you mean?' Jemma shivered, even though the shop didn't seem particularly cold. *It's inside me*, she thought, and tried not to panic.

'You'll probably see later,' said Raphael. 'Now, into the back room with you all. I want to check over this book.'

They followed him in. He laid the tote on the worktop, then took the book out, placed it carefully on top of the canvas, and opened the hard cover. Jemma saw pen-and-ink drawings faded to sepia, and next to them, slanted, reversed writing. Raphael turned another page, and smiled affectionately at it.

'I've seen something like that before,' said Carl. 'This will sound ridiculous, but it was – I think it was on a mouse mat.'

'You're probably right,' said Raphael. 'This is a collection of original drawings bound into a book. They're by someone whose name you probably know: Leonardo da Vinci.'

Jemma, Luke and Carl all goggled at the book. 'This must be worth a fortune,' said Jemma. 'And I've just carried it across London in a canvas bag.' She rubbed her forehead. 'Is there time for a cup of tea?'

A hearty knock at the door made them jump.

'I very much doubt,' said Raphael, 'that there's time for anything.' He closed the book, replaced it in the bag, and walked into the shop. The others followed, and gasped at what they saw. Outside the shop window, London had disappeared. There was only white space; a blank page.

Three more raps.

'Here we go,' said Raphael, and unlocked the door. To no one's surprise, on the doorstep stood Brian.

Chapter 20

'Nice day for it,' said Brian. 'Mind if I come in?' He was carrying a large leather Gladstone bag with shiny brass fastenings.

'I take it this isn't a social call,' said Raphael.

Brian chuckled. 'I'm sure you can work out why I'm here,' he said. He glanced at Luke. 'Still got your new assistant, then?' His eyes twinkled.

'Oh yes,' said Raphael. 'He's doing ever so well. Now, Brian, would you like a cup of tea while I sort myself out?'

'No tea, thank you,' said Brian. He stepped over the threshold and closed the door behind him. His hand stroked the wood as if he already owned it.

'Well, I could do with a cup,' said Raphael. 'And I have fifteen minutes of preparation time.' He strolled into the back room and flicked the kettle on. 'Anyone else want one?'

'Yes, please,' croaked Jemma. Her mouth was dry as a bone.

'And me,' said Carl. 'Here, I'll make it.' He walked into the back room without looking at Brian.

'I'll stick to, um, the usual,' said Luke, getting his drinks bottle from the rucksack which hung on the coat stand. Brian snorted, but turned it into a cough. He sauntered around the shop, peering at the counter, then going behind it and fingering the brown-paper bags on their string. He came out again and ran his finger along a shelf, then inspected it. The only things he didn't inspect were the books. Jemma couldn't take her eyes off him. She felt like a rabbit watching a fox, hoping he hadn't noticed her yet.

'Tea's brewing,' said Raphael. 'I think we'll do this downstairs. I'll join you in a few minutes.'

Brian checked his watch. 'Ten minutes, Raphael. And if you're late, I win by default.' Then he stared as the others walked towards the staircase. 'We're not having *them* in there as well, are we?'

'There's no rule which says that we can't have witnesses,' said Raphael.

'It's hardly fair,' grumbled Brian.

Raphael looked as if he could say many things at this point about what constituted fairness and what did not. But after a second or two he merely replied 'Life isn't fair, is it? Do excuse me.' He opened the stockroom door, and vanished.

Once they had proceeded downstairs with their drinks, Brian surveyed the lower floor of the shop with a

150

professional eye. 'Over there would be best.' He marched to the café area, sat down at a large round table, and stretched his legs out underneath. 'You lot can sit at another table. The last thing we need is you interfering.'

Raphael appeared two minutes later, carrying the now-full tote bag. 'I see you've made yourself comfortable,' he said to Brian.

'Start as you mean to go on,' said Brian. He checked his watch again. 'You cut it a bit fine,' he remarked.

'I'm actually a minute early,' said Raphael. 'Anyone who knows me would tell you that in itself is quite remarkable.'

'Are you ready?' said Brian. He leaned towards the leather bag at his feet, his hand reaching down as he waited for Raphael's answer.

'Oh yes, completely ready,' said Raphael. 'But before we begin—' He studied Jemma, Carl and Luke, sitting at the adjacent table. 'You three must swear that you will never breathe a word of this to anyone.'

They all nodded, silently.

'I mean it,' said Raphael, looking very serious. 'On Folio's life.'

'Oh man, don't make me say that,' said Carl.

'I wouldn't normally,' said Raphael. 'But it's that important.'

At that moment they heard an angry meow, and a ginger blur streaked across the floor. Folio leapt onto the table and Jemma stared at him. He seemed smaller still, more compact, as if he had somehow condensed himself.

'I'm sorry, Folio,' she said. She stroked him, and he

rubbed his cheek against her hand. 'On Folio's life,' she said quietly.

'On Folio's life,' the other two echoed.

Brian sighed. 'It's a ruddy cat,' he said. 'Now, if you've finished messing around, let's get on with it.' He reached down to his bag again. 'I present my first book.' He brought out a large, stout volume bound in ochre leather, and placed it on the table. 'Volume one of Dr Johnson's *Dictionary of the English Language*, 1755. The first dictionary to document the English language properly. I don't think I need to say more.'

Jemma leaned forward. Was she imagining things, or was the book glowing a little?

'A solid opening move,' said Raphael. 'I shall present my first book.' He delved into the canvas bag and brought out the sky-blue book. 'This is a collection of original bound drawings and notes by Leonardo da Vinci.' He set it down in front of him.

'Fancy,' said Brian. 'I take it you won't mind if I verify that.' He opened the book at random, and let page after page fall. A brisk nod. 'Want to check mine?'

Raphael opened the stiff cover of the book, glanced at the title page, and closed it again. 'Looks fine to me.'

Brian exhaled. 'I present book two.' The next book was smaller and clearly ancient; fragile-looking, with uneven yellowish-brown pages. Brian showed a page; writing crosswise over other writing, none of which Jemma could make out. 'May I introduce Archimedes' Palimpsest. You will of course be aware that Archimedes of Syracuse was one of the greatest mathematicians of all time.' Jemma remembered GCSE Maths, and shivered. 'Much of the content of this book was thought to have been lost, and it is centuries ahead of its time.'

'How did you get hold of that?' Raphael asked, quietly.

Brian glared at him. 'Never you mind.'

An eerie glow emanated from the book, and spread to the book beside it. Jemma leaned across to Carl, and whispered as quietly as she could, 'Can you see the books glowing, or is it just me?'

'They're glowing,' he whispered back, his eyes fixed on the books.

Jemma looked at Raphael, her heart in her mouth. What would he bring out next?

Raphael reached into his bag. 'The next one is rather unusual,' he said, and laid a battered book on the table, slightly apart from the first. It had a cover of tooled brown leather, but the design was marred by stains. Raphael opened it, and Jemma saw handwritten pages with occasional spatters and blots. 'This is a recipe book which one of my neighbours has kindly given to me. It contains family recipes handed down through the generations, and is still used in Rolando's café and deli today.'

Jemma's heart sank.

Brian stared at the book, then burst out laughing. 'A recipe book?' he said, grinning. He picked the book up and leafed through it. 'Lasagne? Rigatoni? Tiramisu?' His eyes glinted. 'I suspect you're *trifling* with me.' He let out a hearty guffaw as he threw the book on the table.

'I'll thank you to be careful with that,' said Raphael. 'We respect books, remember?'

'I can't wait to see what you've got for me next,' said Brian. He jerked a thumb at Jemma. 'Her diary, perhaps? Or last week's TV guide?'

'You'll have to wait and see,' said Raphael, very calmly.

He's blown it, thought Jemma. *I could understand the drawings, but – a recipe book?*

Brian looked extremely smug. 'It barely seems worth presenting my third book,' he said, 'but I suppose I'd better.' He brought out one last stout, ancient book, and laid it beside the dictionary. 'This,' he said, 'is a bound collection of writings by Sir Isaac Newton, on a variety of subjects. There.' The book had begun glowing before he laid it with the others, and as Jemma watched the light became brighter still, until nobody, not even the most unbelieving person, could have denied it.

'Nice,' commented Raphael. 'You've been busy.'

'I have,' said Brian. 'I don't go into these things lightly, you know, and I've been preparing for a while.'

'I can see that,' said Raphael. 'Before I present my last book, why did you choose the three books you have?'

Brian raised his eyebrows. 'Isn't that obvious? Words are the foundation of language, and this is one of the best collections of them. Mathematics – well, you can't do a thing without mathematics, and here we have the fresh ideas of a mathematical genius. Followed by the writings of an eminent scientific mind.' He smiled. 'Not even you, Raphael, can deny gravity.'

'I don't propose to,' said Raphael. 'Here is my final book.' He reached into the tote bag for one last time. Then he paused. 'Are you ready?'

154

Brian's smile widened. 'Are you ready to lose?'

Raphael smiled back. 'I think you'll like this one.' He brought out a book which seemed too large for the bag it had come out of; a thick book bound in plain navy blue, with no writing on the cover. He laid it on the other side of the recipe book.

'What's that?' said Brian, leaning over to look at it.

'This,' said Raphael, 'is a bound set of *Popular Science Ideas*, a magazine which presented difficult concepts in a way both children and adults could understand.' He opened the cover, and Jemma saw that inside, just as he had said, was an A4-sized magazine with a brightly coloured robot on the cover. Jemma read the coverlines: *How does manned space flight work? Could measles become extinct? Did the Universe come from a Big Bang?* 'Care to have a look, Brian?'

'No, I would not,' said Brian, his lip curling into a sneer. 'You really have outdone yourself this time, Raphael. How you've kept your position so long I have no idea. Those cheap paperbacks you peddle have gone to your head. What are you, the People's Champion? You should be a purveyor of the finest that has been thought and said, and instead you present me with this – this *trash*. The book of drawings makes sense. But the rest of it—' His chair scraped back. 'I hope you've made retirement plans, Raphael.'

'Not just yet,' said Raphael, and his voice was deadly serious. 'I see you're surprised at my choice of literature, Brian. To be honest, I never expected anything else. The books you have chosen are wonderful, truly wonderful.

They are fine examples of knowledge, and no one could deny that. I knew that would be your approach. That is one of the reasons why I chose to take a different path.'

Jemma swallowed, and leaned forward. She felt Carl do the same beside her.

'My first book,' said Raphael, 'wasn't the one I had in mind. It was even better. I didn't get the book I wanted, but the book I needed. It fulfils the same function, combining artistry, ingenuity, and discovery. The added dimension is that it was chosen for me by a dear colleague, and the transaction was effected by my invaluable shop manager.' He smiled at Jemma, who felt a sudden lump in her throat.

'Who will shortly be out of a job,' said Brian.

'My second book,' said Raphael, 'was again unexpected. It was given to me just this morning. Yes, it is old, it is stained, it has fingerprints all over it, and some of the pages are stuck together. This book of recipes is five generations old. Five generations of culinary knowledge, of improvement, of striving for perfection, all done with care and love. And, moreover, freely given.' He nudged the book across slightly, so that it touched the first, and a gentle, almost imperceptible light appeared. As Jemma watched, it grew stronger.

'My final choice,' said Raphael, 'comes from the library of Sir Tarquin Golightly.'

Brian shook his head in disbelief. 'You had the pick of his library, and you chose *that*?' He pointed an accusing finger at the navy-blue book, and Jemma felt injured on its behalf.

'There are lots of books I could have chosen,' said

Raphael. 'But when I went to visit Lady Golightly, she told me that this was the volume that Sir Tarquin kept on his bedside table. He read the magazines when he was a boy – devoured them, in fact – and those magazines inspired him, against the wishes of his family, to embrace a scientific career. That, and the patents he filed in the course of it, made his millions, and enabled him to restore the family home. He never forgot the magazine, and had it bound to preserve it. In his last illness he would ask Lady Golightly to read him an article every so often, and that was one of the few remaining things that gave him pleasure.'

He stroked the plain blue cover of the book. 'So this book stands for education, for science, for making complicated things comprehensible, and for inspiration and growth.' He paused. 'Lady Golightly refused to take any money for this book. She merely asked me to ensure that it would go to a good home where it would be appreciated and cared for.' He moved the book gently across the table to join its fellows.

This time the change in the light was not subtle, but strong. Luke took his sunglasses out of his pocket and put them on. 'What you don't see, Brian,' said Raphael, his face lit from below, 'is that your ambition has narrowed you. You have specialised, and you have excluded, and you have forgotten that books are not just collections of knowledge. They also foster development, and inspiration, and care, and love. You have collected wonderful books, but in the pursuit of that knowledge you have forgotten to be wise. And wisdom, as you should know, is key.' He glanced at the books, which were shooting out rays of white light. Out of the silence a faint hum emerged. It grew louder and louder, until the table vibrated.

A sudden flash made Jemma cover her eyes and turn away. When she looked back, Raphael's books were alone on the table. Brian's books had gone.

Brian stared at the part of the table where his books had been.

'The books will be taken care of, Brian,' said Raphael. He paused, considering his next words. 'It was a good challenge. You did well.' He held out his hand.

'If that's the sort of drivel you have to spout to win this challenge,' said Brian, 'then I'm glad I lost.' He pushed back his chair. 'I know what happens next, you don't have to tell me.' He walked heavily towards the stairs. Then he turned and glared at them all. 'Don't think you've seen the last of me.' He grinned. 'Did you know you've got a vampire on your team? A bloodsucker?' He pointed at Luke. 'Him, he's a plant. He was working for me. Not that he was any good. Won't use him again.'

Luke took his sunglasses off and stepped forward. 'No, you won't use me again,' he said. 'I stopped working for you as soon as I realised what I was doing would harm good people.' He smiled. 'These people know what I am, and they accept me for it. I'm happier here than I've been for centuries.' He flung up his head. 'Good luck in the outer reaches, Brian. I suspect you'll need it. And don't ever expect my help again.'

Brian snorted. 'Wouldn't want it.' He stomped towards the stairs.

'Better see him out, I suppose,' said Raphael. They got up, and followed.

Brian mounted the stairs, crossed the back room, and walked through the upper bookshop, looking neither right nor left. He paused at the counter, glanced at Raphael, then took out a set of keys and put them down. 'You'll find everything is there,' he said. He opened the door onto the blankness, stepped through, and disappeared.

'You won,' Jemma said, half-dazed. 'Raphael, you won!' She threw her arms around him. 'I can't believe it, and I'm still not sure how you did it, but you won!'

'Yes, yes, I did win,' said Raphael, wriggling as he attempted to free himself. 'I'm very glad that you're pleased. And so am I. I'm not keen on change, as you know.'

'That was intense,' said Carl. He walked over to them, gently removed Jemma, folded her in his own arms, and kissed the top of her head. 'And speaking of change—'

They followed his gaze to where Folio stood in the doorway to the back room. He looked bigger and stronger, like a young lion. He stood proud, his beautiful tawny fur glowing, and his eyes blazed as if they held a light of their own.

Chapter 21

Jemma drifted into consciousness, woken by Elvis Costello on her clock radio singing 'Every Day I Write The Book'. She stretched luxuriously, then jumped as the backs of her hands touched the headboard. *What the—*

Then she remembered. She opened her eyes, and listened to the swishing of traffic in the street below. The traffic on Charing Cross Road.

There had been little time for explanations after Brian's departure. Raphael picked up the keys from the counter, then sent them all downstairs to fetch the three victorious books, maintaining an appropriate distance from each other. When they came upstairs the world outside was just the same as it had always been, and a couple of slightly peevish faces peered in at the window.

'No rest for the wicked,' said Raphael. 'Jemma, would you look after upstairs, and Luke and Carl can go downstairs. As for me—' He picked up the brown-paper bag on the counter and took out the last cinnamon roll. 'If you don't mind, I might go for a nap. I find challenges rather tiring.' For once, Jemma was happy to acknowledge that he had done his bit for the day, and more besides.

Thoughts crashed against each other in her head all through the day, while serving the customers, nipping to the stockroom for books, and fielding questions about Folio's new grooming regime. Folio spent most of the day lounging in the shop window looking mightily pleased with himself, like a predator taking his ease on the plain.

When Raphael came back into the shop, which she noted was five minutes before he usually took his lunch, she checked for nearby customers, then opened her mouth to ask him a question. He held up a hand. 'Not until the end of the day,' he said. And with that Jemma had to be content.

When Raphael had left the shop for lunch, Jemma went to get her phone. Carl had texted: *Are you OK?*

She considered his question. Actually, she felt surprisingly OK, considering that that morning she had fetched a priceless book from a secret library, witnessed an epic battle of knowledge, and also faced losing her job. Typing *Yes, I think so. How about you?* seemed rather mundane, but it was true. Perhaps the more of this sort of thing you did, the more you got used to it.

A reply flashed up on her phone: *It was deeply weird.* Then another text: *Imagine that as a scene in a film or a play. That would be so awesome.*

Jemma smiled. *You'd better get on and write it then!*

It was some time before Carl replied. *Yeah, but would anyone ever believe it?*

Jemma's fingers flew. *Do they have to?* Then she had to put her phone away again, because a customer was waiting at the counter, clutching a book called *Divine Your Future*. 'That looks useful,' she said, and opened the cover. 'Three pounds, please.'

As was always the way with these things, they had a rush of customers at ten to five, and only managed to close the shop at twenty-five past. 'What a day,' groaned Jemma, turning the sign round, locking the door, and leaning firmly against it.

'It was rather, wasn't it?' said Raphael from the armchair, where he had been, he said, thinking for the last hour. Since this involved having his eyes closed and his mouth slightly open, Jemma wasn't entirely sure how much thinking he had managed to get done.

Carl and Luke came upstairs, both worn out. Carl had in fact run out of food at four o'clock, but most of Westminster had needed a late-afternoon caffeine fix. Luke sagged a little, but still looked considerably happier and healthier than he had on several previous occasions. They all gazed at Raphael, who regarded them calmly.

'So…?' said Jemma.

'I've had plenty to think about,' said Raphael. 'I've lost an Assistant Keeper, and gained a bookshop.' He drew Brian's keys out of his waistcoat pocket and jingled them. The keyring glinted: an ancient golden coin.

'Have you made any decisions?' she asked, as casually as she could.

162

Raphael considered. 'I think we all deserve tomorrow morning off. I don't know about you, but I've had enough for one week.'

Jemma sighed. 'That wasn't quite what I meant.'

'Well, I'll have to recruit a new Assistant Keeper,' said Raphael. 'I may need your help, Jemma.'

'Me?' Jemma stared at him.

'Yes, you. You see, the post has never had a proper job description, or a – what is it?'

'A person specification,' said Jemma. Her head was doing the swimmy thing again, but to be honest that had happened so often lately that she was beginning to get used to it.

'That's the fellow,' said Raphael. 'As you know about these sorts of things, you could help me draw one up.'

Jemma giggled. 'For a moment I thought you were asking me to do the job!'

Raphael raised his eyebrows. 'Would you like to?'

'What? But – but – I don't know! I don't know what an Assistant Keeper does, except . . . keep books.' She frowned. 'Anyway,' she added, 'you ought to follow proper recruitment procedure, not just ask the person standing in front of you.' She folded her arms, feeling on considerably safer ground.

'What will you do with the shop?' asked Luke. Jemma shot him a grateful look, glad that he had asked the question occupying her mind.

'I suppose there are two options,' said Raphael. 'Sell it, or keep it. It's a nice little shop, really. I'd take you round, but it's best to let the shop settle first. Let's give it till after

163

the weekend.'

'Is it another magical one?' Jemma asked.

'I expect so,' said Raphael. 'I'm not sure *how* magical, though. For obvious reasons, Brian was never particularly open about the place. It's a bit odd: it's a fairly modern building, but Brian's made it very olde-worlde. All mahogany shelves and brass fittings. It's a bit like being on an old ship, or perhaps in a coffin-maker's.'

Luke's face brightened.

'Yes, it's rather a pleasant shop,' said Raphael. 'And probably pleasanter now that Brian's out of it. So yes, I shall keep it. So long as I can get someone to run it.' He shot Jemma a speculative glance.

She studied him, trying to work out what was behind his expression. 'Do you want me to draw up a job description and help you recruit a bookshop manager?' she said.

Raphael laughed. 'Not this time. I wondered how you'd feel about managing it. I'll still need you here sometimes, obviously, but Brian does have an assistant, and I'm hoping she'll stay on. She is capable, if a little gloomy.'

The pleased expression flickered over Luke's face again.

'Really?' exclaimed Jemma. *My own bookshop*, she thought. *Really, actually, mine to run!* Then another thought struck her like a sudden shower of icy water. 'I don't think I can,' she said. 'I don't know anything about antiquarian books.'

'You'll find Maddy very knowledgeable on that front,' said Raphael. 'In any case, it doesn't have to be an antiquarian bookshop. It could be any sort of bookshop.'

Jemma's mouth dropped open, then she nodded frantically. 'Then yes! Yes, I'd love to!'

'Jolly good,' said Raphael. 'If you can get here for say eight o'clock on Monday, we'll go and take a look at things.'

Brian's bookshop, BJF Antiquarian Books, had been much as Jemma imagined: wood, brass, leather-bound books behind glass doors, and no prices on anything. Maddy, Brian's assistant, was a tall, thin, lugubrious woman in capri pants and Birkenstocks, with a long thin plait of dark hair which looked as if she had chewed the end of it. She had taken Brian's departure with equanimity, and Jemma had a feeling that Maddy expected her to be more of the same. She didn't think she would be – she didn't think she *could* be – but for now she was watching, and learning, and inspecting the books in the small stockroom which smelt as old as time.

And she lived above the shop. 'There's no point in not using it,' Raphael had said. And when they went upstairs they found a large, beautifully furnished open-plan living and eating area, and in the eaves of the building, a bedroom with sloping walls and a surprisingly luxurious ensuite bathroom.

'It's beautiful,' said Jemma. 'How much rent will you ask for?' She had a feeling that, given the location and the furnishings, she might need to ask for a pay rise.

Raphael smiled. 'Call it a benefit in kind,' he said.

After some misgivings that the flat and the shop would have malevolent intentions towards her, Jemma eventually

165

plucked up the courage to bring over a sleeping bag and camp out. She spent the first night on the chesterfield sofa in the living room, worried that she would offend the place if she dared to use the bed. She had lain awake flinching at the slightest noise, eyes wide open and darting about the room every time a shadow moved. But she must have slept, for she woke at seven o'clock exactly feeling surprisingly refreshed. She rushed to a mirror to check that she hadn't been turned into a frog or developed a horrendous rash overnight, and only then admitted that perhaps Brian's shop might be a little easier to manage than Raphael's.

After five nights of more or less peaceful slumber, during which she had braved the big double bed, Jemma had given notice on her own flat. She had begun to move her belongings over bit by bit, until Raphael laughed when she came into Burns Books with a toaster, ordered her to pack her things, and turned up on Saturday afternoon in Gertrude. As Jemma carried her last possessions out of the flat and closed the door behind her, she saw that the B on the door wasn't crooked any more. She rolled her eyes and walked away.

And there had been changes at Burns Books, too. She had asked Luke what would help him to work in all areas of the bookshop, and between them they had sourced a clear sunlight-filtering film which Luke said would repel the rays which he found most irritating. Once they had applied a large square to the shop window, his sunglasses only appeared on very sunny days, which were becoming rarer as the year rolled on. They had also installed a table and chair in the stockroom, so that he didn't have to eat standing up. Now Luke looked almost healthy, and Jemma hoped that the pigeons in Trafalgar Square were living easier lives.

Yes, all in all, thought Jemma, *things are going rather well*. And today was her regular morning at Burns Books. She got up, got ready, and started to cook breakfast. Four eggs scrambling in the pan, four slices of toast in the toaster.

At eight fifteen precisely, her doorbell rang. Jemma answered the intercom.

'It's me, Carl. I was, um, passing, and—'

'I'm just making breakfast,' said Jemma. 'Care to join me?'

'Sure,' he said, and she could hear his smile.

This was the third day in a row that he had called in on his way to work. They ate at the round dining table, with proper, heavy cutlery, but Jemma drew the line at damask napkins, and set out the paper ones with watermelons on that she had brought from her flat.

'That was lovely,' said Carl, wiping his mouth. 'Want to walk down with me? You are in our shop this morning, aren't you?'

'I'd love to,' said Jemma. Once they were downstairs and she had locked the door, he held out his hand and she put hers into it.

It was a short walk to the bookshop. Fallen leaves crunched under their feet, and they laughed at their dragon breath in the chilly October street. The lights were already on at Burns Books, and Jemma saw Luke behind the counter, priming the till. Carl stole a quick kiss before diverting to Rolando's for their pastry order. Jemma watched him stroll down the street, then pushed the bookshop door open.

'Morning,' she said. 'All OK?' She could see it was, but she still hadn't got out of the habit of asking.

'Oh, yes,' said Luke, and grinned.

'I'll be down shortly,' called Raphael, from somewhere overhead. 'Just, um…'

Jemma was wondering what strange ensemble Raphael would present himself in today when a stentorian meow jolted her out of her thoughts. 'You're in good voice, Folio,' she said, bending to stroke the cat's luxuriant fur as he weaved in and out of her legs. She wobbled slightly as he pushed between them, and giggled. 'Careful!'

Folio looked up at her, and his amber eyes glowed. Then she tickled him behind the ear, and he purred with pleasure. *It must be lovely to be a pampered cat in a bookshop*, she thought. *Then again, working in one isn't bad, either.* And as Carl came in with the trays of pastries, she smiled a big, warm, happy smile.

Acknowledgements

My first thanks are for my marvellous beta readers – Carol Bissett, Ruth Cunliffe, Paula Harmon, and Stephen Lenhardt – and my fantastic proofreader, John Croall. As ever, thank you all for your feedback – and yes, I am getting on with book three!

An additional thank you goes to my husband Stephen for his support and encouragement. Apologies that I don't seem to be able to write any faster!

My final thanks are for you, the reader. Thank you for sticking with the Magical Bookshop series, and I hope you enjoyed this instalment of the bookshop's adventures. If you did, a short review or rating on Amazon or Goodreads would be very much appreciated. Ratings and reviews, however short, help readers to discover books.

FONT AND IMAGE CREDITS

Cover and heading fonts: Alyssum Blossom and Alyssum Blossom Sans by Bombastype

Book: Vintage books vector by macrovector_official at freepik.com: https://www.freepik.com/free-vector/books-set-black-white_4352249.htm

Cat (flipped and cropped): Cats silhouettes pack vector by freepik at freepik.com: https://www.freepik.com/free-vector/cats-silhouettes-pack_719787.htm

Coffee cup: taken from Cafe and coffee house pattern vector Free Vector by rawpixel.com: https://www.freepik.com/free-vector/cafe-coffee-house-pattern-vector_3438011.htm

Sunglasses: taken from Cool sunglasses in retro design free vector by freepik: https://www.freepik.com/free-vector/cool-sunglasses-retro-design_757374.htm

Stars: Night free icon by flaticon at freepik.com: https://www.freepik.com/free-icon/night_914336.htm

Chapter vignette: Opened books in hand drawn style Free Vector by freepik at freepik.com: https://www.freepik.com/free-vector/opened-books-hand-drawn-style_765567.htm

Cover created using GIMP image editor: https://www.gimp.org

About the Author

Liz Hedgecock grew up in London, England, did an English degree, and then took forever to start writing. After several years working in the National Health Service, some short stories crept into the world. A few even won prizes. Then the stories started to grow longer...

Now Liz travels between the nineteenth and twenty-first centuries, murdering people. To be fair, she does usually clean up after herself.

Liz's reimaginings of Sherlock Holmes, her Pippa Parker cozy mystery series, the Caster & Fleet Victorian mystery series (written with Paula Harmon), and the Maisie Frobisher Mysteries are available in ebook and paperback.

Liz lives in Cheshire with her husband and two sons, and when she's not writing or child-wrangling you can usually find her reading, messing about on Twitter, or cooing over stuff in museums and art galleries. That's her story, anyway, and she's sticking to it.

Website/blog: http://lizhedgecock.wordpress.com
Facebook: http://www.facebook.com/lizhedgecockwrites
Twitter: http://twitter.com/lizhedgecock
Goodreads: https://www.goodreads.com/lizhedgecock
Amazon author page: http://author.to/LizH

Books by Liz Hedgecock

Short stories
The Secret Notebook of Sherlock Holmes
Bitesize
The Adventure of the Scarlet Rosebud

Halloween Sherlock series (novelettes)
The Case of the Snow-White Lady
Sherlock Holmes and the Deathly Fog
The Case of the Curious Cabinet

Sherlock & Jack series (novellas)
A Jar Of Thursday
Something Blue
A Phoenix Rises

Mrs Hudson & Sherlock Holmes series (novels)
A House Of Mirrors
In Sherlock's Shadow

Pippa Parker Mysteries (novels)
Murder At The Playgroup
Murder In The Choir
A Fete Worse Than Death
Murder in the Meadow
The QWERTY Murders
Past Tense

Caster & Fleet Mysteries (with Paula Harmon)
The Case of the Black Tulips
The Case of the Runaway Client
The Case of the Deceased Clerk
The Case of the Masquerade Mob
The Case of the Fateful Legacy
The Case of the Crystal Kisses

Maisie Frobisher Mysteries (novels)
All At Sea
Off The Map
Gone To Ground

The Magic Bookshop (short novels)
Every Trick in the Book
Brought to Book

For children (with Zoe Harmon)
A Christmas Carrot

WHITE
RHINO
BOOKS

Printed in Great Britain
by Amazon

75756020R00106